Diamond

RARE GEMS SERIES BOOK 2

By

KATHI S. BARTON

World Castle Publishing, LLC

This is a work of fiction. Names, characters, places, and incidents are products of the author's imagination or are used fictitiously and are not to be construed as real. Any resemblance to actual events, locations, organizations, or person, living or dead, is entirely coincidental.

WCP

World Castle Publishing, LLC
Pensacola, Florida

Copyright © Kathi S. Barton 2013
ISBN: 9781629890456
First Edition World Castle Publishing, LLC December 15, 2013
http://www.worldcastlepublishing.com

Licensing Notes

Cover: Karen Fuller
Editor: Eric Johnston

Chapter 1

Diamond was exhausted. She'd worked three doubles in a row and now all she wanted to do was to go home and soak for three days in her deep tub. She thought about using the hot tub that Blair, her new alpha and brother-in-law had had installed just a few days ago, but worried he and Sapphire, her sister would want it and she'd be there feeling stupid. Diamond was getting her things gathered up when one of the doctors came into the lounge.

"I was wondering if you'd stay for another half shift." Diamond was already shaking her head. "Please? There's been an accident on the highway, and I need all the nurses I can get. There are four cars involved. I will pay you triple time if you stay."

She tried to tell herself she didn't need the money badly enough to be dead on her feet for her three days off. She started putting her things back in her locker when Doctor Jan Talley walked over and hugged her.

"I'm not doing this because of the money but because I'm off for the next three days and if you call me, I will say no. I'm too tired to work a good shift as it is now, and I need these days off. Promise me you won't call me." Jan nodded. "I want you to say it. I will feel a great deal better if you do."

"I promise I won't call you even if it's just me working the shift." Jan hugged her again as she continued. "I wish I had more nurses like you and your sister. I'm telling you right now that you and Ruby are the very best I have."

Diamond didn't disagree with her because she knew that she and her sister were the best. The others were just there to draw a check so far as she could see, and she and Ruby were dedicated. They loved what they were doing, and Ruby was going to make an amazing doctor as well.

The first ambulance rolled in ten minutes later. The woman had a broken arm as well as a head trauma, neither of which was life threatening. The man with her had some abrasions, nothing that needed attention, but you'd have thought he had lost his arm the way he was going on and on. Diamond had had enough.

"Shut up." He looked at her, stunned. "You go out there in that waiting room and don't move until I tell you to. And if I hear one peep from you, I'll come out there and show you what pain is."

He moved toward the door just as Jan came around the curtained area. If she'd heard what Diamond said to the man, she didn't say anything to her but looked over the woman and sent her up to be x-rayed.

The next ambulance had two men, both in serious condition. One man had been the driver of a limo. He'd been hit in the driver's side door, the medic had told her, and had slammed his head hard against the window. She was cleaning off his head wound when the other man that had come in with him staggered around the corner.

"Is he going to be all right?" he said. She didn't know and told him. "He's with a limo service here in town. I would like for someone to contact them. Would that be all right with you?"

"You should go back to the bed, sir, and let the doctor look at your wounds. I think someone will call for you." She didn't have any idea if they would or not, but the man nodded. "I'll be over there soon and have a look at you."

"No. Stay with him." His tone made her think that he was used to having his orders obeyed, but she wasn't in the mood to be ordered around by someone who was obviously hurt.

"Get your ass back in that bed and stay there. You're taking precious time from the other injured people by acting like some macho dickhead." He looked at her with a surprised look. "I'm not kidding you. Either get in that bed or so help me, I'll put you there myself."

He was chuckling when he went back around the curtained area. Diamond had to take several deep breaths before she could continue with her job. The man on the bed moaned slightly when she took his blood pressure, and she told him she was sorry. Two more nurses came in an hour later and helped her prep the limo driver for surgery. An hour after that, she was going to the other bed.

He didn't say anything more to her, but she could feel him watching her every move. The smell of blood was making her lightheaded, and she realized that she'd not eaten anything in the past fourteen hours. Her plan had been to have some leftovers at the house and get into bed.

"You should know that I'm impressed by you. Not many people would speak to me the way you did." She ignored him and cleaned the large wound on his leg. She'd even taken great pleasure in cutting the expensive suit from him. He continued talking while she assessed his injury.

"I was wondering if I could make a phone call. I think my phone was lost sometime after the accident. I called nine-one-one, and after that I don't remember what happened to it." He smiled at her as she waited on the doctor to tell her to stitch him up. She closed her eyes for a second, felt herself sway a little, and popped them back open.

"Your girlfriend will have to wait. There are no public phones in here for you to use." She sat down on the room's only chair and had to steady herself against the counter before she fell off it. "If you give me a number, I'll make sure she knows where you are."

The room was spinning. She felt sick. She had no idea what was going on, and when arms wrapped around her, she leaned into the strong male chest that held her. Diamond didn't even have the strength to lift her head to see who held her.

"Come on, breathe for me." The man on the bed was holding her. "Come on now, you can't pass out on me, who would I have to sew me together again?"

"Let me go." He didn't, of course, and she felt herself being lowered to a bed. "I can't lay here. Let me up."

She didn't have it in her to struggle with him. Then she heard him laugh again. He was saying something that made no sense to her. Then she heard another voice, one she was too tired to make out. But her body began to realize it was in a good position and it was going to take advantage of it. Sleep rolled over her like a freight train. Soon she was out.

~~~

Thad watched the young woman sleep. He had noticed that she was exhausted when she'd been looking at his driver. He might have stayed and teased her more into arguing with him if he hadn't seen that she was close to falling over. Thad looked up when someone entered the room he'd asked to have her moved to. He was pleasantly surprised to see Sapphire and Blair.

"Thad? What are you doing here?" Sapphire went to the bed as Blair shook his hand. "I thought…Christ, were you in that accident?"

"Yes. We were nearly to the turn off on the highway when the car in front of us suddenly just flipped over. I'm sure there was more than that, but it's all I saw when Jasper slammed on the brakes, tossing me to the floor." He looked over at the two women, just now realizing that they were related. "Your sister is a nurse?"

"Yes." Sapphire brushed back the hair that had fallen over the woman's cheek. "She has worked three doubles this week and was supposed to get off over seventeen hours ago. She called and told me that she was staying, but that she was getting off ten hours ago. They are very short staffed here."

"Apparently. She looks like you now that I know the connection. She passed out in my arms and I had them bring her in here. I've been in here with her since someone stitched up my leg." He looked down at the white bandage that covered most of his calf and knee.

"You'll stay with us until you're ready to leave." Blair didn't make it sound like a request, and Thad had to laugh a little. If he didn't know any better, he'd swear that the nurse was related to both of them.

"I was told an hour ago that Jasper, the driver, didn't make it. And that seven people were killed out there. Do you know what happened?" When Blair looked at Sapphire, he knew that they didn't know either, but before he could ask, the woman sat up suddenly.

"Oh God, I'm going to be sick." Sapphire helped her move off the bed and to the bathroom. Both he and Blair stood there watching as the door was opened and both women disappeared into what appeared to be a bathroom.

"She's been working for eleven days straight. It's a small wonder she'd not passed out before now. We've been trying for a week to get her to tell them no, but she won't." Blair sat in the other chair and smiled at him as he continued. "I'm sure she's going to tell me that she will take some time off, but I'm betting that she won't. Too much like her sister in that respect."

"What's her name?" He had no idea why he wanted to know. "She tore into me earlier when I told her to take care of Jasper. Spit fire little thing, isn't she?"

"Diamond, and she's been known to hold her own." Blair stood up when the door opened again, and there stood the two women. When Thad started to stand, she glared at him. What he wouldn't give to see if she had that much passion when making love.

The thought had come from nowhere and he was a little startled by it. He had never had those kinds of thoughts about women that had been as rude to him and as mouthy as she'd been. He stood anyway just to see her get pissy again. She didn't disappoint him.

"What is wrong with you? Sit down before you open your wound again. I swear to you that I've never seen a man so bent on hurting himself." She moved to the chair behind him and shoved it under him. He had no choice but to sit. "Blair, will you see if I can stay until this moron is released?"

Before he could tell her that he'd been released while she'd been napping, Blair snapped at her. "You'll get your ass to your locker and put your stuff in my truck. I'm not allowing you to work another minute more looking—"

The low growl from Diamond had all of them tensing up. Thad watched as Blair took a step back when Diamond moved toward him.

"You listen here, you big, overgrown pup. I will do as I damned well please, and you'll learn to live with it. You do not *allow* me to do squat, do you understand me? I'm a grown woman."

"Then act like it." Thad hadn't realized he'd spoken out loud until she turned to him, but it was too late now. "You've passed out in my arms, puked what little there was on your belly up, and can barely stand up without holding onto someone. If you don't want people to treat you like a childish brat, then don't act like a kid without a nap and do what you're told."

She took a step toward him, and he stood up. He felt his wound tear open, but he wasn't going to back down from her. She looked…delicious was what came to mind, and he wanted to taste her fiery lips as much as he needed his next breath. When she stood there glaring at him for what seemed a lifetime, he took a step toward her, only to have her take one step back.

"I don't like you."

He grinned, thinking if that's all she had he was going to have a great deal of fun with her.

"Most people don't. Actually, I think that other than your sister and her husband, no one does. Not even my own family."

"I can see why. You're bossy and stupid with this self-proclaimed power that you think everyone should just jump when you say so." He wanted to test her theory about him and have her kiss him but was actually afraid she'd hurt him. "I'm not one of your minions."

"No, you're not. One of my *minions*, as you called them, would never have spoken to me the way you have and gotten away with it. I'll have to think of a proper punishment for you. Maybe I could think of something while I'm recuperating at your home."

Diamond jerked her gaze to Blair so quickly that he wanted to laugh. The man looked like he he'd been pinned to the wall. And Thad had a feeling that whatever he had planned for the little nurse wasn't going to be anything compared to what she had in store for the big man she was staring down.

The door opening behind her had Thad want to shove her behind him to protect her. He had no idea where that thought had come from either, and was worried he might have hit his head harder than they all thought. He was just about to ask the doctor that when she turned on Diamond. He was glad now that he was there to see this, because there was no way he would have believed it if anyone would have told him.

"You should have told me no when I asked you to work extra. Now I'm down one nurse because you had to get sick in the middle—"

"I told you no. Repeatedly, as a matter of fact. And also the day before that and the day before that too, if you'll remember correctly, when you asked me to work double shift after double shift. And today you said that I'd only work a half a shift after you'd begged me to work another double today. I was here for nearly nine hours after that supposed time to get off." Diamond moved toward the doctor and had her backed up against the door. "You can kiss my ass. I quit."

The doctor looked around the room as if she had no idea what had just happened, and she was still standing there when Diamond shoved past her and into the hall. Sapphire was moving to go with her sister when the doctor, Talley he thought her name was, finally came back to herself.

"She can't quit." Blair nodded when she looked at him. "There is no reason for her to get all upset over this. I was...I was just worried, that's all. I usually get pissed off, then I...she didn't really quit, did she?"

"I'm pretty sure she just did." Blair helped him gather up his things as he continued talking to the doctor, who still looked like she'd been pole axed. "She'll need to make arrangements to gather her last check I would assume. And there had better be no problems with it, or so help me I'll own you and this hospital at the end of the day."

Thad had never seen this side of Blair Henson before. He'd always been so laid back and easy. This man was hard yet quiet in his demands, and Thad had no doubt that they were demands either. And apparently neither did the good doctor.

"I'll make sure it's correct. But I'd like to talk to her. I'd like to tell her how sorry I am and that I'd very much like for her to reconsider her quitting. She's the best nurse I have."

"Then you should have thought before you spoke." Blair turned to her then and smiled. It wasn't a friendly smile, Thad realized. It was actually sort of scary. "Don't fuck with my family, doctor, and I won't your job. Leave my sister-in-law alone, both of them."

"You think that Ruby will quit too?" The panic in her voice made Thad think that Blair was a great deal more of a big deal around here than he'd ever realized. The man simply oozed power and obedience. Thad found he wanted to please the man as well, and he wasn't even on the receiving end of his anger.

As he was wheeled out, he began to think of ways to get back at the pretty little nurse. The *unemployed* pretty little nurse. There was something very appealing about her, and he wanted to explore the things that made him want to get to know her better. Smiling, he looked up at Blair.

"What if your sister-in-law were to take care of me when I'm at your home? You know, see to my wound and help me around? I'd be more than glad to pay her." He tried to look innocent but was sure he was failing. "I could also see the next set of plans that you and Sapphire have for me while I'm here."

"It'll be up to her, but I got the feeling she didn't care for you overly much." Blair looked at him hard, and Thad had to work at not squirming under such scrutiny. "She will more than likely give Talley another try, but I can't for the life of me see why. The woman would suck her dry if Diamond let her."

"I don't know, Blair. I have a feeling Diamond is a great deal stronger than she looks. I'm betting she could take her on without much in the way of trouble." He smiled when he thought of the sponge baths he was going to receive from the girl. "You think she's any good at chess? I would love to find someone to challenge me in a few games while I'm here."

He'd been introduced to strip chess when he'd been in college. Back then it had been a way to get a girl naked without having to buy her dinner first. He and his roommates had been really good at it too, and it had gotten him the reputation of being quite the player, in more ways than one. Thad was sliding into the truck when he realized he didn't even know if Diamond was seeing anyone. Not that it mattered, he supposed. He just wanted a good time, nothing long term was in his future if it involved love and women. Never again.

Chapter 2

"So help me, if you say that to me again, I'm going to pop you in the face when I get there." Diamond looked at the man standing in the line at the grocery. He'd been arguing with someone on the other end of his phone since she'd walked up behind him five minutes ago. She looked around to see if anyone would open another lane so she could get out of the way when this guy blew his top. All she wanted to do was pick up some ice cream and go home to eat the entire container while feeling sorry for herself. She'd never been unemployed before, and she was going to enjoy every second of it. This wouldn't be all that long. At least she hoped not. Just long enough for her to talk Doctor Talley into letting her come back to work.

"There is no fucking way that I'm going to put up with your shit any longer." He turned and glared at her as if whatever was going on was somehow her fault. "You had better have your shit out of my house by the time I get there, or so help me, hell will be paid. And all by you."

She was never sure when someone was finished with a call when they used an ear device and were actually talking to her or still in conversation with the person on the phone. So when he snapped his fingers in front of her face several times, she was startled enough to take a step back. His laughter did nothing for her horrible mood.

"You know, you really should be aware of your surroundings when you're talking on one of those things. Perhaps I didn't care to hear you arguing with your friend, and I might have found your use of language offensive." She watched as his face turned a nice shade of purple before she continued. "And for your information, snapping your fingers in front of my face will get the shit knocked out of you someday too."

"Fuck off, bitch. If you didn't like the conversation, perhaps you shouldn't have been listening. And it's a free country last I looked, so I can say what the fuck I want, when the fuck I want to. So fuck you." She smiled at him and thought of all the things she'd like to do to him if he pushed her just a little more. "Women like you, all uptight and coldhearted, shouldn't be out among others like me. You need to find a man and get fucked. You might feel better."

Over the limit, her mind screamed at her, but she took a step back. But when he pressed his finger to her forehead and told her to get a clue, it was not only over the limit, but had raced the fuck over the finish line and into the next realm. Her fist came out and connected with his face so fast she'd not even realized she'd hit him until he started screaming like a little girl. Then someone called the police. And when they arrived fifteen minutes later, her mood did not improve.

"Miss Erickson, I'm sorry, but Mr. Caldwell said you hit him without any provocation." She looked at the police officer who was standing between her and the man she'd hit. Several times as it turned out.

"Who's Mr. Caldwell?" He nodded toward the man that had pissed her off. "Oh. I didn't know what his name was. But as for no provocation, I'd say that's a false statement. He called me names, and when I tried to back away from him, he punched his finger into my forehead and told me to fuck off. And he called me coldhearted and said I needed to get laid so I could feel better.

Actually, what he said was I should find a man and get fucked. Then I'd feel better."

She heard someone laugh behind her but didn't turn as they put Caldwell into the other ambulance. Diamond had had enough of people today and wasn't going to engage in any more verbal disputes. She looked at the officer, who she only just realized was a wolf when he suddenly stiffened. He quickly told her she was free to go. She just knew it was going to be Blair or her sister behind her. When the large hand pressed against her shoulder, she was actually relieved to know it was Blair and not Sapphire. But that was short lived when Thad spoke.

"Perhaps you need to enroll in anger management classes." She heard Blair tell Thad to hush, but the stupid man seemed to like egging her on. "Or maybe some yoga. You might benefit from a few classes that show you creative ways to channel your anger."

"He told me to get fucked and I'd feel better." The hand on her shoulder tightened and she had to put her hand over Blair's before he hurt her more. "He also called me a bitch, which, actually I am, but what really made me take offense was when he said I was coldhearted." She stood up to leave when she was pressed back into the gurney she was sitting on. Blair handed her the ice pack that had fallen from her cheek. Thad pulled it away when she tried to cover her face with it.

"Did he hit you?" She nodded at Thad and felt the tears threaten again. "Where is he?"

"He was taken away when they figured out I'd broken his arm. I told him not to grab me again, but he just wouldn't listen." She looked up at Blair, who was still holding onto her arm. "I'd very much like to go home now. The police said it was okay for me to leave as soon as you got here. Can you take me home?"

"Come on, baby." She was helped to stand by Blair and felt Thad standing a little too close to her. She wondered what he was doing there when Blair told her. "I was taking him back to the hotel where his things were so he can stay at the house. He was in the truck when Sapphire called me."

She nodded. Well, she supposed, he really was staying at the house. He'd better stay the hell away from her or he'd really be hurt. Stretching her neck, she tried to calm her wolf. She'd been pissy with her since she'd left the hospital. When she climbed into the backseat of Blair's truck, she leaned her head back and closed her eyes. It had been one hell of a day, and it was only three in the afternoon.

Diamond must have fallen asleep, because the next thing she knew, she was being shaken awake. Twice she tried to push the person away, and both times she was told to wake up. When she finally did open her eyes, she was staring at Thad. He was smiling at her like he knew some secret.

"You snore." She pushed at him when he spoke. She most certainly did not snore. "You do. It's sort of a soft purr, but I don't think you're much of a cat. I don't know why, but I see you more of a...I don't know, something that would tear a man apart if he pissed her off."

He had no idea. Blair and Sapphire had decided to tell Thad what they were but hadn't as yet. It's not that they didn't trust the man; he'd paid them when he said he would and had given them the best contract that Blair said he'd ever seen. Everyone was happy with him. Diamond hadn't met him until today and now she wished she'd been able to postpone that event for a while longer...like forever.

"Would you mind backing up? I can't get out with you hovering over me like some sort of stalker." He laughed but moved out of her way. She looked over at Blair when he chuckled at her too. This was becoming the worst day of her life. She got out of the truck and moved to the house, ignoring the men, and only stopped in the kitchen long enough to give her grandmother a kiss on the cheek and tell Allen, Blair's father, hello. She needed a bath and a long night's sleep. She was nearly to her room when she heard her name called. Turning to look at Thad, she wondered what it was about him that made her want to lash out at him every time he said anything.

"Do you need someone to scrub your back?" She nearly went back down the stairs and showed him a thing or two about what she needed, but turned on her heel and moved the rest of the way up the stairs. She was going to need therapy after this was finished.

She was pulling her hair up into a thick ponytail when she heard the knock at the door. She groaned and nearly told the person to go away when she realized it was her grandmother.

"I brought you something light to eat. Blair said you had some ice cream, but it's all melted. I'll get you some tomorrow if you want." She nodded at her grandmother and picked up the slices of cheese and some crackers. "I've been fielding calls too. Doctor Jan Talley has called here several times begging to speak to you. What would you like for me to tell her?"

"Tell her I'll call her tomorrow. I've been thinking I was stupid in quitting like that anyway." She walked to the tub that was filling and turned off the taps. "I shouldn't have let myself get exhausted like that. It's my fault, not hers."

"I don't think so, but then you're the one that has to work with her." She stood up and left her the tray. "Sleep until you wake, dear. You're off for the next few days and you should enjoy it."

Diamond soaked in the tub for nearly an hour, refreshing the water occasionally just to keep it warm. By the time she rolled out of it, she was as limp as a rag and had eaten all but one cracker and two slices of cheese. After drying off, she crawled into bed, wondering if she needed to set her alarm, but closed her eyes and let sleep take her before she even picked her phone up to set it. Her last thought was of the arrogant ass Thad and whether or not he was going to be all right in the morning.

~~~

Thad discovered three things his first morning in the big house. First, and probably most importantly, he was not used to women in large groups. The Erickson women, including the grandmother, were not a group he'd want to deal with on a daily basis, especially not in the morning. Secondly, they didn't drink coffee, and no matter how much he begged them, no one would help him get a cup. Third, and now that he thought of it this should have been first, he was not in as good of shape as he'd thought he was. There were five flights of stairs to any point in this house to get to a bathroom and five more to come back down. He was dying and decided that a treadmill was in order. And where the hell was Diamond?

"Would you like to go into the office with me now or when Sapphire comes in after she takes care of her clients?" Blair leaned down to him and whispered in his ear. "I'm going to Tim Horton's on the way into work, and Sapphire won't."

"You. I'm going with you." He glanced up at the door when it opened and was disappointed not to see Diamond. All the other women were there, but not her. He had some major teasing to do, and she wasn't there for him to have his fun. He was hobbling toward the door when he heard one of the sisters say her name. Thad tried to look like he wasn't eavesdropping, but he was, and he was pretty sure Emerald knew it when she winked at him.

"I took her phone last night after I knew she was asleep. She didn't even stir. I did cover her up though. I didn't think sleeping naked without at least a sheet was such a good idea, as tired as she was." Thad tried not to swallow too loudly, but the thought of Diamond naked was nearly too much for him to imagine. "She's going to go back to work for that bitch, I just know it."

Thad knew that Emerald didn't care for the doctor. In fact he got the impression that none of them did. Especially Ruby, who was only going to be a nurse as long as it took her to get out of med school and become a doctor.

"Well," Jade said as she pulled on her boots, "she'll do what she feels is right and not what we think. Diamond needs to be a nurse as much as I need to work outside. And today is the big day."

They both moved off, and he had a moment to wonder what the big day was about, but Blair had moved to the door to leave, and Thad needed his coffee. They were in the drive-thru lane when Thad finally asked about Diamond.

"She's all right, isn't she? I mean she did almost pass out, then that thing with the guy at the store. She's not going to get sick, is she?"

Blair ordered before he answered him. "Nah, we seldom get sick, but exhaustion is pretty serious, and Diamond was beyond that. I think she worked for an entire month recently without a day off before she finally put her foot down. Sapphire thinks that woman that runs the hospital knows that Diamond won't say no to her, and takes advantage." He handed him his plain black coffee before he continued. "Diamond was offered a great job at one of the bigger hospitals recently, and we're actually afraid she'll take it. We don't want her to move away."

Thad had noticed that even though they fought a great deal, he knew that they were very close. He'd never had any sisters, and only the one brother, but he'd not seen him in so long that Thad sometimes forgot he had one. He and Ward had never been all that close and had drifted even further apart after their mom died a few years ago. He didn't even know where he'd gone after he'd kicked him out of his house. He glanced over at Blair when they pulled into the parking garage at Flair Marketing. He decided to try and find him; just find, not contact, he thought after a moment.

"What would I have to do to find someone that I didn't want to know I was looking for them? I have a brother that I'm curious if he's still alive, but don't want him to come near me." He had no idea why he thought Blair would know, but when he nodded at him, Thad felt better just by asking.

"I have a few contacts that I can use. Mostly they work for the police department, but I can get something started for you." They entered the building together, and Thad was given a badge and was told it was his to use every time he came to Ohio. "That'll get you in and out of here when you need to. If you lose it, I'll have to murder you in your sleep."

Blair was standing at the elevator when Thad realized the man was kidding. He hoped he was, anyway. He could deliver a line like the one he'd just said to him without blinking an eye. He vowed never to play poker with this guy. He'd lose his entire billions in less time than he could play a hand against him.

Blair wasn't ready for him to meet the staff, so Thad was set up in an empty office. He was even given a secretary to help out.

He was on a call to his foreman when Sapphire walked in. She smelled of dark coffee, and if that was what she had in her hand, he was going to kiss her. She set the cup in front of him and sat down. Even the strong smell was giving him a rush.

He hung up on Morton. Morton Guzman was going to drive him crazy over this new production line. Thad knew he'd have to go back to Texas and fire the man before this was all done, there was just no help for it. Thad took a sip of his coffee before speaking to Sapphire. She seemed to understand his need for it this early.

"Morton said that the specs you sent him are all screwed up and he has to redo everything." He raised his hand when she started to speak. "I've already told him if he changes one thing on those mock-ups I was going to personally come down there and rip his ass open."

"As I've suggested before, I think he needs to be put elsewhere on this project. I believe he's responsible for the delays we're having now." Thad nodded as she continued. "And the guy is a bully. I can't believe how he talks to his secretary."

Thad hadn't realized that until Blair had told him while he and Sapphire were visiting three months ago. Sapphire had overheard her crying in the ladies' room and had talked to her. She'd gotten the entire story from her and then some. Apparently she was leaving the company because of other issues, but since she wouldn't say what, he had no grounds to fire Morton, more's the pity.

Thad leaned over and rubbed the wound on his leg. It was burning again. He had looked at it this morning when he'd gotten in the shower and was surprised at how red it looked. He was going to have to call the doctor when he got home.

"You should have Ruby or Diamond look at that. It might be infected." He looked at Sapphire when she spoke. "We can't afford to have you ill."

"I'm fine. And Diamond might cut my leg off just for spite. I don't think she cares for me overly much." Sapphire just smiled. "How is she? I didn't see her this morning before we left."

"Still sleeping. I checked on her before I left and she hadn't moved." She paused for several seconds before she continued. "What do you think of my sister?"

If there had ever been a more loaded question, he'd never heard it. He leaned back in his chair and waited for her to clarify what she was asking him. When she didn't, but instead continued to stare at him, he changed the subject. He was so not going to go down that path.

"I have a new product that I'd like you to have a look at. It's what we talked about before with the drinks. I have someone from one of the manufacturers of the milk and juice companies coming here day after tomorrow. Do you think you can work with them?" She nodded. "Mike is kind of an ass but smart. Caroline is all business, so you'll like her too."

"Send me what time they'll be in and I'll work them in." She stood up, and so did he. "Diamond won't be easy. She's been hurt before, badly. And if you hurt her, I think you know that I'll hurt you."

"I do. And I have no intentions of hurting her. She just...there's something about her that I find intriguing. But I'm not going to do anything with her or to her that she won't consent to. I'm not that sort of person." She nodded and moved toward the door, but stopped and turned to look at him.

"What does she smell like to you?"

He answered her without thinking about it. "Meadows in the summer and dark rich chocolate. Why?"

She smiled and left him to stand there. He had no idea why the way Diamond smelled would concern her sister, but he wasn't used to women like these. Thad wondered why she didn't just ask her sister what perfume she wore and not him. He sat back down and starred at the computer for ten minutes before he started to work. But by noon he had to go back to the house. His leg was killing him.

Chapter 3

Annabelle was worried about the young man. He was limping more and more as the afternoon wore on, and now he was sweating. She had called Ruby, but she was in the middle of something and said she'd call her back, but that had been over an hour ago. It was time to wake Diamond and have her look at him. But since he'd already refused to go to the doctor, she decided to play him.

"I was wondering if you could go up and see if Diamond is awake yet." He stared at her with glassy eyes, and she knew he was running a fever too. "She should be up by now and I could use her help with the garden."

"I can help you." She shook her head, and he glanced at the stairs. "You think she's awake and not coming down then?"

"I think she might be awake, yes, but I'm afraid she might be sulking." Annabelle hoped Diamond would forgive her the lie. Diamond did not sulk, she got even. "You know she quit her job, and that man at the store upset her too."

He nodded and moved to the stairs. She almost felt sorry for him but knew that once Diamond got a look at him she'd know what to do. Annabelle hated to wake her, but she was worried about Thad.

The phone rang just as she was putting the cake for dinner tonight on the cooling racks. Chocolate with buttercream icing was just what they needed. She answered it on the fourth ring, and was glad to hear from Emerald finally.

"The exams were a breeze. I'll be home tonight if the rain holds off. Grandmother, I think I'm going to take the job at the grade school. I'll be close to home and have the grade I want. Second graders are so awesome." Emerald giggled. "That is if I passed my tests. I think I did well but you never know."

"You did just fine. I just know it. And when you get here, we'll have a big dinner tonight. I just baked a cake and we'll have steaks on the grill." Emerald moaned. "I thought you'd like that. Be safe and call me when you pull over for gas or a break. Don't forget to walk around too."

After Emerald assured her she'd be careful, they hung up. Annabelle was going out to the garden when she realized that she should wait to see if Diamond came down and needed her. She looked up the stairs, then at the clouds. If she waited, there would be no fresh green beans for dinner and she was looking forward to them. Annabelle decided to chance upsetting Thad for her garden. Laughing, she hoped that he'd get the care he needed and not piss off Diamond so much that she'd hurt him worse. Her granddaughters were nothing if not a little on the violent side when pissed.

Smiling, she saw Allen coming out of the shed with a basket and a hoe. The man loved gardening as much as she did and had been extremely helpful with it this year. They had already talked about doubling the size of the garden next year and opening a little stand. They had big plans for such old people, she thought.

"I was just coming to see if we were picking or not today." She nodded at him and took the basket. "I've been thinking of these beans since you said last week that we could pick them about now."

"Well, let's see what we can get. Emerald is coming home if the rain doesn't stop her." She was so involved in her garden she never worried about her granddaughter or the man she'd sent up there. Annabelle knew he'd be all right.

~~~

Thad had to stop three times to catch his breath. He was sure now that it had little to do with the shape he was in and more to do with the wound. It was pulling, and he hurt. He knocked several times on the door he was told was Diamond's and went in when no one answered. He couldn't have been more surprised by what he saw than if someone had told him an elephant were in here.

The big bed was a four-posted canopy that looked to be made of solid oak. The lacy canopy looked like it had been handmade a long time ago. He moved into the room, stood at the foot, and looked down at the woman there.

"Christ," he whispered when he saw her. Her back was bare all the way down to the dimple at her ass. He wanted to move the thin sheet to the side and see if there was another one to match the one he could see. Thad reached up to the wooden bar that held the canopy in place and crushed the lace in his hand when he thought about what other treasures she had beneath her.

Forgetting about his leg, he reached down with an unsteady hand to touch her. Thad needed to know if she was as silky and as smooth as she looked. Touching his finger to her spine at the nape of her neck, he ran his finger down her slowly and nearly moaned himself when she did. Just as he touched the sheet that covered her bottom, she shifted on the bed and it fell away.

There was a matching dimple. Not only that but she had a beautiful birthmark in the shape of a heart just below it. Thad didn't just want to see more of her, hell, all of her; he needed it. Curling his finger into the sheet to pull it back, he stopped. When she stiffened beneath his touch, he looked up. He could see her confusion, but he thought he saw a spark of need too.

"What are you doing?" Her voice was low and husky. Thad gripped the rod tighter as he felt his cock harden incredibly more. "Thad?"

"Roll over for me. I need to see you." She stretched out and pulled the sheet over her as she moved to her back. "I want to see you. All of you. Pull the sheet down for me."

He watched as it inched down. He wanted to beg her to pull faster, but was enjoying the slow move too. When the sheet seemed to catch at her nipple, he whimpered. They were just there, and he was going to see them. But she stopped and he looked at her again.

"You're not supposed to be in here. I was sleeping." He nodded, just short of begging her to continue. "I think you should leave now."

"I want to see you. Show me please." She shook her head and pulled the sheet up higher. Thad whimpered as she sat up and pulled the sheet completely over her. "You're beautiful. Very beautiful."

Diamond lay there, staring up at him, and he moved to sit on the bed. For as much as he'd forgotten about his leg while he'd been trying to sneak a peek at her, it was hurting all the more now. He either sat on the bed or fell on it. Either way, his leg was no longer going to hold him up.

"What have you done?" She pulled the sheet tighter around her and moved toward him. Thad saw the expanse of her back again but was hurting too badly to appreciate it much.

"I think it's infected or something. That woman who put the stitches in said that it looked dirty to her but she'd been told to sew it, not clean it. And no amount of begging her to have someone else do it would work." Diamond shoved him back on her bed and told him to not move. That wasn't going to be a problem, he was fucking hurting too much to do anything more than breathe right now.

When she dropped the sheet as she moved to the bathroom, he knew the sight would be burned in his memory for the rest of his life. Christ, she was more beautiful than he'd ever seen, and he couldn't wait to have her beneath him...and the sooner the better. She came back dressed in an old jersey and not much else. She also had a large first-aid kit.

"You'll have to stay still and let me pull out the stitches. I'm sorry, but all I have here is some topical numbing agent. I'm afraid I can't do much more than that." He nodded, suddenly feeling sick. "Look at me, Thad. Now, look at me."

He opened his eyes, not even realizing that he'd closed them. She was so close to his face that he wanted to pull her the last inch and kiss her. But he was afraid if he did, she'd not help him.

"I'm going to cut away your pants. Are you okay with that?" He nodded. "And I'm going to have to get permission from Blair to help you. I'm sorry, but I have to...there is only one way I can heal you, but I have to get permission first."

"Beg him. Tell him I'll pay him any amount of money he wants. Just please make it stop." When he thought he saw her lick his leg, he decided that he'd become delirious. There was no way anyone would do that. He nearly exploded when she moaned somewhere near his cock. "Diamond, you do know that I'm a desperate man, don't you? If you lick my cock like that, I'll buy you the prettiest nightie I can find and let you model it for me."

Thad felt her move him on the bed. He must have helped her some, but his mind was still playing tricks on him, because he was sure she hadn't lifted him up. When he heard the sound of his pants tearing, he reached down to cup his cock. He was as hard as stone.

"Behave or I'll make Blair do this." He grinned at her distressed tone. "You're going to...hurt yourself if you keep this up."

"I like to give pain, love, not receive it. Though for you I'd give it a try. I'd very much like to see you strapped to my bed and take a small whip to your backside. Would you like that?" She said something, but he knew this was his dream and he made her agree not tell him to fuck off. "I'd tie you on the hump too. Fuck your pretty little ass until you begged me to let you come. Christ, I hurt."

Thad drifted in and out of his fantasy. At one point, he would swear there was a large wolf in the room with him, but he knew that couldn't be true. Dangerous too. He felt his body being lifted again, but before he could open his eyes, even if he could, he was drifting off again.

The next time he opened his eyes, he shut them tight. The room was bright, and when someone laughed, he decided that he'd become a vampire and only live in darkness.

"Won't do you any good to become a vamp after this. You're well on your way to becoming something else. Besides, I'm not sure how Blair would like you crossing over. And I'm pretty sure you've stepped beyond that point." He looked at Jade when the room became darker. "Welcome back."

"Where...?" His throat was so dry he could barely speak, but she gave him a straw and he sucked the finest nectar in the world down, water. When she pulled it away before he had nearly enough, he wanted to beg her to give it back.

"Diamond said for you to take it easy when you woke up. She said you'd feel like shit, but you should be on the mend sooner than normal. How are you feeling?" Emerald moved a book to the table near her and sat up in the chair. "You gave us all a scare there for a while. Good thing Diamond helped you when she did or it could have been bye-bye Thad."

"How long have I been here?" Thad tried to sit up but was just too weak. He felt as if he'd been run over by a truck, a car and a train. All at once. He looked up when he realized she hadn't answered him.

"Five days. You passed out on Diamond on Monday and today is Friday. Though it's really late on Friday." She grinned at him. "Don't you remember anything?"

He started to tell her no, but then he remembered the conversation he'd had with Diamond about playing. He hoped that he'd been only dreaming, but he had a feeling that he'd been very vocal about his wants and needs. He started to ask Emerald what she knew, but she answered his question before he could ask.

"Diamond said you were out of your head for most of her fixing you up. She won't tell us what you said but blushed every time someone asked her. I'm thinking you have a thing for my sister and you might have told her." She leaned forward in the chair and wiggled her brows. "Do you have a thing for Diamond?"

Thad decided that no answer was going to be right, so he kept his mouth shut about what may or may not have passed his lips when he'd been sick. "I had a few people coming into town, do you know if they have been postponed or not?"

Emerald laughed as if she knew that he'd been changing the subject just to avoid answering her. But she continued on as if he didn't do just that. "I think you might have embarrassed her. And she doesn't embarrass easily. Did you enjoy yourself?"

"Emerald, behave." Thad looked at Diamond, who stood in the doorway. "Why don't you go and tell Grandmother that Mr. Galloway is awake now and would probably benefit from some of the broth she's made for him."

Diamond stood still while her sister left the room. He wanted to ask her what he'd said to her, but she'd called him Mr. Galloway and not Thad, as she had before. When she moved toward the bed, he could see the stiffness in her and wondered how badly he'd screwed up with her.

"I was talking out of my head before." She nodded and pulled his wrist to her and took his pulse. He was sure it was elevated, because he couldn't get out of his mind the way she'd looked when he'd arrived in this room.

"You're going to need to get up and moving. You'll get pneumonia if you don't, and I'd very much like to have my bed back." Thad wanted to offer her half of it with him still in it but kept his mouth closed. "I'll have Grandmother bring you your cell phone up too. It's been ringing like crazy, and we've kept it charged for you."

Thad nodded and realized she was leaving him again. "Stay please. I'd like to…I think I might have said some things to you that I shouldn't have. At least not until we get to know one another better."

"We won't. Be getting better acquainted, I mean. I have enough on my plate right now." She fussed with a bag hanging on the back of the door before she turned to him again. "And you didn't say anything important, if that's what you're thinking."

Anger pulsed through him for a split second, and he directed it at her. "I think I offered to buy you a sexy nightie and tie you to my bed. Are you telling me that you've no desire to have either one? I can assure you that I'm a very generous Dom if my sub is a good girl."

Thad saw it. It was quick and hot, but she was interested. He wanted to try out something on her, anything, but right now he was too weak to make her obey or punish her if she were to disobey him. And Thad found he really wanted her to disobey him.

"I don't…I don't play, Mr. Galloway. I don't think…I know that if I did, you'd be the last man on earth I'd want to do that with." She was out the door before he could form an answer. She didn't slam the door behind her, she might as well have for all the effort she put into not slamming it. Laughing, he leaned back on the headboard and thought about little Miss Diamond all pinked up from his hands and paddle. He had a raging hard-on and no relief in sight when Annabelle came in a few minutes later with a tray and his cell phone.

"I'm sorry I can't stay but I've another pie in the oven. I've been experimenting with some of the fruits I picked up at the market." She set the tray over his lap and smiled. "Will you be all right until I can get back up here? Just call the house phone if you need me. I've written it down on the pad there."

She was gone before he could thank her. Looking down at the food on the tray made him think she had brought him his dinner too, but when he put the first spoonful of the rich broth into his mouth, he had to have it all. He didn't think there had ever been a better meal.

He must have dozed off, because when he woke, his tray was gone and there was a pile of his clothes lying on the chair next to the bed. He took the note off the top and read it.

"You should want a shower about now, so if you feel like an adventure, call downstairs and I'll come up and help you. Later. Blair."

He stretched and felt pretty good, so he decided to take a shower on his own. He got up slowly because he wasn't stupid enough to think his leg was as well as it felt and stood up. He was naked, he realized, and wondered if Diamond had undressed him. His cock started to dance a little, and he had to have a stern talk with it before he moved to the bathroom.

"She's made it perfectly clear that she's not interested in us. Not that we won't try and convince her otherwise, but for now we have to be good." He stroked his cock, thinking about her being naked with him. "She's lovely and oh so ready for us."

He brushed his teeth as the water warmed up in the stall behind him. He was feeling a little weak but nothing he couldn't handle. Thad stepped into the spray and thought about his leg and leaned down to have a look at the wound he had gotten in the accident. He nearly fell over when he saw that it was gone.

"Not healed but gone." He closed his eyes against the sound of his voice and stood there while the water sprayed over him. He looked down twice more just to be sure, but he was right the first time, there was nothing there, no stitches, no wound and not even a scar.

Scrubbing his hair with the only shampoo he could find made him think of Diamond again. Christ, the woman was everywhere. But he remembered he was in her bath and things were bound to smell like her. He found himself taking the bar of soap to his nose more times than was necessary as he finished up. By the time he was finished scrubbing his body for the second time he knew he was going to need some help to get out and dressed. But the problem was, he was all alone and his phone was in the bedroom. What a fucking moron he'd turned out to be.

"Hello?" He heard the voice yet couldn't believe it for a few seconds. "Are you in here, Thad?"

"I'm in the shower." Thad was going to triple Blair's pay if he'd help him out of this situation and never mentioned it again. When the hand came around the curtain and turned off the water, he nearly wept. The towel being shoved in next made him want to cry like a five-year-old.

"I thought you'd call me. When Diamond heard the water turn on, she said you'd be stuck in here. After forty minutes of water running she had me come up here." He heard the laughter. "I'm not going to repeat what she said about you, but suffice it to say, she's not very happy with you."

"She never is." He wiped the towel over his chest, then wrapped it around his waist. He pushed back the curtain to find

Blair in the bathroom with him, but his back was turned. He'd never been so grateful to someone in his life.

"She's a bit on the intense side, but then all the Erickson women are. Diamond is a good nurse and knows her stuff. She said you'd be too stubborn to ask for help, and I guess she was right." Blair handed him back a pair of boxers. "Sit on the toilet. Once you have those on I'll help you with the rest. I like you and all but not really all that much."

"Same here." By the time he was completely dressed, he wanted a nap again. He also wanted to ask about his wound, but couldn't hold his head up any longer. While he'd been in the shower with Blair, someone had made the bed, complete with fresh linens. As soon as his head hit the pillow, he was out.

Chapter 4

Diamond wasn't having any luck finding a job. Not that she wasn't getting offers; she was getting those, just not any she could bank on. By the time she was driving back to the house, she'd decided that she'd have to take the job back at the hospital. As much as she hated working for Talley, she needed a job more.

"Nothing yet I take it." She looked at Grandmother and shook her head. "Something will come along, you'll see. Why don't you go in the dining room and I'll bring you some lunch? You deserve a nice treat."

She moved into the room after kissing her grandmother on the cheek. She stopped in the doorway just as she saw who was sitting there. Diamond did not want to fuck with Thad today. Before she could back out, her grandmother pushed her the rest of the way into the room and told her to have a seat.

"Diamond didn't have any luck finding a job today, so I invited her to have something to eat with us." Grandmother sat a plate in front of her. "Thad was just telling me that he's going into the office today. He was asking me about you."

"Why?" Diamond flushed when her grandmother raised a brow at her. "I mean, why is he asking about me? I'm not doing anything with him. For him, I'm not doing anything for him."

Thad laughed, and she felt like getting up and punching him in the face. When her grandmother stood up to answer the phone, Diamond glared at Thad.

"What are you still doing here? Your leg is perfectly fine." He laughed as he picked up his sandwich but didn't answer her. She pushed the plate back and glared harder.

"You do know that you'll need your strength for me, don't you?" She flushed deeper as she remembered what he said he was going to do to her the other day. "I'm remembering a good deal more of what I said to you, and I'm thinking you're going to love everything. Including the nipple clamps. I ordered them for you yesterday."

Diamond felt her nipples harden in her bra and shifted on the seat. The man was nuts if he thought she was going to play in any games with him. She started to stand up when he did as well. They were nearly touching, and he reached out and tugged her to him by cupping the back of her head.

His mouth was so close that she could see his beard coming in. She wanted to touch him, to pull him closer to her, but she was suddenly afraid to. She knew what this man was to her and had been doing her best to avoid him. Now it looked like she was going to have no choice. When he took a step back, she nearly reached for him, but she heard her grandmother coming and moved out of the way of the door for her.

"I just got a call from that man of yours again, Thad. He seems to be under the impression that he can speak to me as if I'm some underling of his. I set him right." She looked around the room at the two of them. "What's happened? Diamond, have you told him yet?"

"No." She started to move out of the room when Thad said her name. "I don't want to talk about it. It's not that important. Not to you at any rate."

"How about if you let me be the judge of that." She heard the steel in his voice, but was too overwhelmed by him to be cautious of it. She turned when he snapped her name again.

"I said it's not important. I made sure you were going to be all right despite what I know I should have done. You didn't lose your leg, and everything is just peachy." She moved back when he took a step forward. "You'll need to stay away from me. I'm not kidding. I will hurt you if I have to."

"Sit down." She had forgotten about her grandmother being in the room with them. "I said for the both of you to sit down right now. This is not how we treat one another in this house."

She continued standing. She wanted out of this room and out of this house before her grandmother said something that would have him asking questions. Questions she was sure would make it so she'd have to tell him he was her mate. And though it had been hard, she'd kept that from everyone else in the house but her grandmother, and she wasn't going to tell him.

"What is it about my leg that you fixed?" His voice was calm, but she could feel his temper like it was her own. Taking his blood into her body was doing that. She glanced at her grandmother, hoping she'd come up with something.

"You have to tell him love. He has to know or you're going to be hurting long before he finds out on his own." She shook her head. "Sit down and…. Damn it."

She left them for the phone again. Diamond was shocked to hear her curse; her grandmother wasn't one for a potty mouth as she called it. As soon as the door closed behind her again, Thad stood up and moved toward her. She could see the intent on his face and was almost as much afraid of what he had in mind as him finding out she was a wolf.

She pressed herself against the wall, but he moved closer still. When he was within touching distance, she whimpered and felt his touch on her arm. She looked at him and saw that he was angry still, but he wanted answers too. She moaned when he touched her.

~~~

Thad moved slowly. For as much as he wanted her to tell him what was going on, the need to touch and be touched by her was driving him over the edge. Her scent, too, one he was sure didn't come from a bottle or from soap. This time when he pulled her to him he didn't let her pull back.

"I want to taste you. Then I want to take you upstairs and fuck you. What better way to spend a hazy afternoon than getting sweaty between the sheets?" She pushed at his chest, but he didn't let her go. "If I'm barking up the wrong tree, Nurse Ericks—"

"I don't bark, Mr. Galloway, I howl. And I'd appreciate it if you'd simply back the fuck up. I don't want your attention or your speculations on what I should do with my spare time." When she moved to walk away from him, he reached for her arm. He wasn't used to people not doing what he wanted and she...intrigued him. But when he touched her, he hadn't counted on her strength and found himself pinned against the wall, dangling a foot from the floor with her hand around his throat holding him there.

"You're lovely when you're pissed off." Thad's head banged hard against the wall in a short hard punch. "If you hurt me badly enough, will you nurse me back to health? Please?"

"Put him down, Diamond." Thad knew the voice and the man. "Now, Diamond, put him down."

Her low growl had Thad's cock harden immediately. And when his feet touched the floor, he watched her face, looked deep into her eyes, and was startled to see a wolf there.

His coat was black, almost blue and shining brilliantly. That's when he realized the wolf was a female and he wanted to stroke her. He licked his suddenly dry lips.

"What are you?"

"Nothing you can handle." Before she walked away, he pulled her to him and twisted around so that she was pressed against the wall where she'd held him. Need coiled deep within him. Overwhelming and surprising, he wanted to take her right here, right now. Leaning down to her mouth, her breath, hot and sweet, heated his already overheated body. Kissing her was all he could think about.

"Let me in, Diamond. Please, I need to taste you." He didn't wait for an answer, but kissed her, taking all she had whether she offered it or not. And he tasted paradise.

She growled low again, and he tasted it, felt it. Moving his leg slightly, he moved his thigh between hers and heard her sharp breath when he lifted her against his hardness. Before he could continue, feel more of her, he was suddenly torn from her and sitting on the floor.

He didn't move, fear replacing the need. He had no idea why he was suddenly afraid of Blair, but he was pretty sure it had a lot to do with the way hair seemed to sprout over his body. Dark fur moved so fast over his skin that he was sure it had been his imagination. Maybe he might be able to convince himself of that later, but he was still sitting here, and fur still seemed to be dancing along the big man's body.

When Blair took a step toward him, he knew he was going to die, but Diamond put herself between him and Blair, and then he was afraid for her. Before he could stand, Sapphire seemed to come out of nowhere.

"What the hell are you doing?" Thad opened his mouth to answer her but realized she was speaking to Blair. "Didn't I tell you this was going to happen? Didn't I tell you several times, I might add, to stay out of it?"

"He was kissing her and...he had her...they were nearly having sex. Against the wall." Diamond flushed bright red when

Sapphire looked at her. But Blair wasn't finished. "You should have seen the way he was groping her."

"Like you do to me whenever you get the chance?" Thad laughed but covered his mouth when Blair and Diamond glared at him. He wasn't sure which was scarier at this point. Sapphire told him to get up.

"Now, we're going to do this rationally and as adults." Sapphire pointed to the table, no doubt expecting them all to sit. Well, he wasn't ready to sit. He wanted to get the hell out of this house and…and do what, he wasn't sure.

"I'd do what she says or she'll make your life a living hell. She's already pissed because of Morton." Blair took the chair at the head of the table as he continued. "You should know that we meant to do this under better circumstances. But things have…progressed to the point where it's a need to know rather than a maybe you should know."

He sat but wasn't happy. "What has he done now? So help me if he's done anything to this project I'm going to fire his ass right now. He seems to keep forgetting that he works for me, not the other way around."

Thad nearly pointed out that they did as well but thought now wasn't the time to bring this up. Something was going on here, and he thought he was going to need this information if they were this set on him having it. These people he trusted. Thad looked at Diamond when she sat as far from him as she could.

"We're wolves, werewolves as a matter of fact." Thad waited for the punch line to Sapphire's joke, but she nodded and then looked at Blair as he picked up the story.

"I'm the alpha to our pack, and Sapphire is my alpha bitch. Actually, she's as much alpha as I am, but we run this pack together. All of her sisters are as—"

"Hang on. You're seriously expecting me to believe that you're werewolves? That you sprout fur once a month and hunt down humans for food?" He stood up and sat down quickly when he thought of the wolf he'd seen in Diamond's eyes, as well as the fur on Blair's body. "This can't be happening. There is no such thing as werewolves. Next thing you'll be telling me is that there are vampires in the world."

"There are." He looked at Diamond when she spoke. "There are two of them on your night shift and one on your day staff. She's a half breed. I met her when I went to Texas to visit Sapphire for a few days."

"Prove it." No more than the words left his mouth than Diamond stood up and changed. He was afraid to move when the large wolf made its way around the table and toward him. And when she stood up on her hind paws and put her front ones on his lap, he watched as she opened her mouth for him and showed him those sharp canines.

"Diamond, that's enough. I think he believes you. Go shift and get dressed. But I expect you to come back here." The wolf dropped to the floor and moved around him again to do just what Blair had told her to do. Thad watched her leave the room and continued watching the door for her to come back and tell him it was all a joke. But one look at Blair's face and he knew that this was no joke.

"Diamond nursed you back to health when your leg was infected. Licking your wound of all the poison was all that saved you." Blair nodded at Sapphire, not really hearing what she was saying. "Do you know what a mate is?"

"A pair." She nodded. "I saw her. The wolf. When I was ill. I thought I was hallucinating or something. She healed me because a dog's...wolf's mouth is cleaner than a human's. How the hell does someone find this shit out?"

"Only another super would know what each of us are. And yes, a pair. But when she took your blood, she formed a connection with you. One that was already there but not formed.

When I asked you the other day what she smelled like, I thought she was your mate, but I wasn't sure. Now, after today, I'm sure of it." Sapphire took his hand and he jerked from her. He knew that he'd hurt her, but right now he was too close to freaking out.

"Diamond is a wolf too then." Blair nodded as Sapphire left the room. "I hurt her. I'm sorry for that, but I can't…why did you feel the need to tell me today. Why at all?"

"Sapphire told me you were Diamond's mate, and then this morning Annabelle said the same thing to me. I can't make you want her, but she's your other half." Thad burst out laughing. "I'm sorry that this is making you uncomfortable but—"

"Uncomfortable? We've gone the hell over uncomfortable and are closely coming up on fucking freaked out. I nearly had sex with…with that." He felt the surge of anger from Blair but didn't really fucking care right now. "I guess I can be glad that you told me before I stuck my dick in this."

He looked at the doorway when he heard her. Thad had no idea how long Diamond had been standing there, but by the look on her face, long enough to hear him. He wasn't going to apologize to her. She'd known all along what she was and had let him…well that wasn't right either. She'd been pushing him away since he'd been there. Thad stood up when she disappeared.

"I need to get back to Texas. I have some things going on there that I need to…we have a contract, are you…fuck, I have no idea what I want right now. I'll…I'll call you in a few days." He wasn't going to call him at all but have his attorneys handle this. He just knew that he wasn't going to be working with these…people any longer.

Thad made arrangements for a cab to come and get him, and he waited outside until it arrived. His things were brought out by Annabelle, who simply set his luggage and his computer on the picnic table and went back inside. She looked as hurt as he was pissed.

Once he was at the airport, he felt a little better. Distance, he supposed, was a big help, and once he made it home again they'd be out of a job and he'd have to start over. But the more he thought of it, the angrier he got. He wondered if he could sue them. Then he caught himself. Yeah, that would go over well. *"I can't work with them, your Honor, because they're werewolves and they said I have a few vampires working for me too."*

Every time his phone rang he ignored it. He wasn't in the mood to speak to anyone right now. And when his flight was called he turned it off and took out the battery for good measure. He was going to enjoy his flight home.

Thad had called his house to have his car brought to him. On the ride back, he pulled out his phone and started to sort through his voicemails. The first one he listened to was from Morton.

"I'll be changing shit back to the old way in the morning. Glad you finally came to your senses about them people and their wanting you to convert. That Henson woman sure was bossy, but I'm glad you fired her. We'll get back to normal now."

Thad had no idea what he was talking about until he got to the third message. This one was from Blair's attorney.

"As per the contract signed between Flair Marketing and Galloway Industries, we are in agreement with the break in the contract. You'll receive official notifications in the mail in the morning as I am over-nighting the information to you. I have stated that there are creative differences that cannot be overcome. If you have any questions regarding this, please contact my office and not the firm."

Thad was livid. How dare they do this to him? He was going to break it with them, of course, but he should have been the one to do it, not them. He listened to his next message and nearly froze on the spot when he heard her voice. Diamond had left him a message.

"You left some things in my room. I don't want you to think I've stolen them, but I will have them cleaned and pressed before I have them sent. You'll not have to worry about my...." She let out a long breath before she continued. "They'll go out within the next few days."

She'd been about to tell him that her germs or some other part of her wasn't going to be on whatever it was she was sending him. He wanted to call her back and tell her not to bother, that he could replace whatever it was, but he wasn't ready to speak to any of them just yet. He moved through his house and to his bedroom, where he took a long hot shower. Tomorrow he'd deal with all of this; right now he was exhausted and emotionally worn out. Tomorrow would look better.

Chapter 5

Diamond put the last of her boxes in the back seat of her car and closed the door. She looked at her sisters and her grandmother and wanted to cry again. But this was what needed to be done, and she was sticking by her decisions. The hospital in New York was going to be a good place to begin again. If she got the job. No one knew it wasn't a done deal and she was keeping it that way.

"Are you sure about this?" Jade asked. Diamond nodded. "I don't want you to move away. This is our home, we're family."

"I know, but I need to have a job, and this one is the best." It was also far away from Texas, which was the point she supposed. "I'm going to be working a great deal, but I promise that I'll call all the time. Every day. You won't even miss me."

She'd made the decision after leaving the message for Thad. She had sat in her bedroom and sobbed over his shirt, and had even put it on. Stupid now when she thought of it, but she'd been so hurt by him that she'd wanted to send his things back smelling like her. But he was just a human and he'd not smell anything anyway and put it in the laundry. Then she went into her bathroom to take a long bath and smelled him in there as well. Everything, including her own clothes, smelled like him, and she decided to leave. She had dropped off his shirts and pair of pants at the dry cleaners that morning.

It took her all night to pack up her things. Then after everyone was gone for the day she took it all out to her car and started loading it in. Her grandmother must have put out a call because, within half an hour, they were all back at the house to try and keep her from going. The only person who didn't say anything was Blair. He just helped her carry the things down the stairs. But after they all hugged her and went into the house, he leaned against the car and looked at her.

"Will you ever forgive me?" She looked at him, startled by the question. "I fucked this up for you, and I'm sorrier than I've ever been in my life. I should have let you handle telling him in your own way."

"He wasn't going to take it well no matter how he found out." She looked at the woods instead of Blair as she continued. "I'm not going to say that I'll come back here, but I'd like to be welcome in the pack if I do."

"You know that you will be a part of my pack for the rest of your life. And you'd better come back here. Sapphire will be pissed at me if you don't come back when we have a baby." The pang of her sister having a child ran deep in her heart. "Diamond, let me try to fix this, please? You know what will happen to you if you don't at least talk to him."

"I may not turn rogue, and we both know it. He didn't do anything more than kiss me, and I helped his wounds. I'm pretty sure in a few weeks I won't even remember what he looked like." Neither of them believed that, and she was sure they both knew it. "Besides, you'll be rolling in the dough once you get this product off the ground. You and Galloway Industries will be contenders."

"After he left here, I contacted our attorneys and told them to dump the contract. We can't do business with him, and I'm pretty sure he would have done the same thing once he got back to his home. Sapphire and I are going to see if we can market it to someone else in six months." Diamond felt the tears fall. "Don't cry, baby, it's for the best. He'll either come to his senses or not, but either way, we came out ahead on this. We have a product that we know will sell."

Diamond was just getting into her car when another car pulled into the drive. Two men got out and came toward them. She had a feeling that Galloway Industries wasn't going to go quietly into the night.

"Mr. Blair Henson of Flair Marketing?" Neither of them said a word as the men looked down at their notes. "We're here to see Blair Henson. Does he live here or not?"

Blair stood up and let a little of his wolf go. Diamond watched the other man as he took a step back. Before either of them could move, the first man pulled a gun. Blair pushed her behind him.

"We only want to talk to Henson. If you're not him then I would suggest that you simply say so and we'll go up to the house." The click of something had them all turning, and Diamond saw Emerald standing there on the deck with a gun pointed at them all.

"You'll either lose your dicks or your brains. I'm thinking they're both in the same general area so it's entirely up to you two who gets it first." Sapphire came out on the deck then with her phone to her ear as Emerald continued. "My sister is calling Galloway now, and Grandmother is calling the police. I'm pretty sure that if you were told to pull a gun on my family, you're all going to jail. But I'm thinking it'll be just you idiots."

"He said you'd be pissed off, that we were to protect ourselves if need be." The man who spoke seemed to be happy at the turn of events, but all she could think about was this was really stupid. She looked at all of them and decided enough was enough, this had to end now. Diamond put out her hand to take the gun from the man, and he jerked back and pointed the gun at her. She heard the shot before she felt the pain. And by then she was falling. What the hell had just happened to her?

~~~

"See if you can get a meeting set up with the foremen at the plant. Tell them that I...." The pain was incredible. Thad doubled over and held his belly in hopes that it would pass, but it only grew more intense. He was sure that he'd been shot, but when he pulled his hand away, there was nothing there but skin. Trying to stand up, he felt the world spinning out of control, and then the floor came up and slapped him in the face. Blackness swallowed him up and he thought of Diamond in those last seconds.

"Don't move," his secretary said. Thad sat up anyway and looked at his secretary. She looked like she'd seen a ghost. "Are you all right, sir? You scared me to death."

Thad had been terrified as well, and when he stood up, he felt weak and out of sorts. Moving to his desk slowly, wondering for a moment how he got in his office, he looked back at Jane. She flushed brightly and stood up from her kneeling position on the floor near his couch.

"You fainted. After you screamed and then fainted I called security and they helped me put you in here. When we couldn't find anything wrong with you, I called the doctor, and he said you were more than likely exhausted. He said you were sleeping and not hurt." She moved to his desk and handed him a stack of messages. "Those came in right after you fell. The man, Blair Henson, he said for you to call him as soon as possible the first few times, then...well, then he said never mind when he called the last time. He said it was no longer important."

Thad almost just tossed the messages in the trash but saw Diamond's name there. "What happened, did he say? Did he mention Diamond Erickson?"

"Yes. At first, like I said, but then after...." She stopped when he glared. "Mrs. Henson called first and asked about us sending out some goons. I assured her that we didn't work that way. Then Mr. Henson called back a few minutes later. He was screaming something about her being shot and that you were a...you were a son of a bitch who'd shot her. I told him that you'd been here all morning, and he said something about some henchmen. I wasn't sure what he was talking about, so I hung up. The next time he called back he was calmer but no less abusive. He certainly didn't seem like the man who called the first time. He was...well hell, he acted like his world was ending. He's the company you're doing business with on the veggie containers, right? I can't wait to get them. I think—"

"Can you reach him for me?" Jane nodded and moved to the door, but he stopped her. "Never mind. Could you just get my plane ready to go to Ohio? I need to...I have to see what is going on."

The longer he sat there thinking about Diamond the more he thought something had happened to her. He didn't have a clue about henchmen, but he did know who might. He picked up the phone and called Morton. For some reason, Thad thought he was behind all this.

"Henchmen, you say? Nope. Did send out my son and his friend to tell them to back off. Did you know that they're planning to sell your idea to another firm? Heard tell they are saying it was all theirs." Thad buzzed Jane as Morton continued. "I haven't heard back from him since he was there, but I'm guessing he's made some progress."

"It was their idea." Putting the phone on speaker, he waited for Morton to say something as he wrote out a note to Jane. He needed to get to Ohio more than ever now, and he wanted her to set up an appointment with Blair as soon as possible.

"Well...I suppose that we can say that it was yours, and nobody will be the wiser. I'm willing to say whatever you want for a price." Thad looked up at Jane as Morton unknowingly spewed more information to them both. "Otto, my son, he's got himself a gun down there. I told him to be careful of them people. They ain't anything more than dogs with big teeth, but then ain't we all at some point."

He knew. That's all Thad could think of was that Morton knew. And according to a conversation he'd had with Sapphire before leaving, only another supernatural would know about another one unless they were told. That made Morton a sup. But what?

He had to be slick, trick him into answering him. But how? He waited, knowing that sooner or later this was going to come back to bite him in the ass, but he had to take a chance.

"One of them is my mate." There was silence both in his office as well as on the phone. "Diamond. Diamond Erickson is my mate, and we've bonded."

"Mother fuck," Morton exploded. "You have to get rid of her. That's the only way. Mother…you say you've bonded? Shit, let me call Otto back and have him hunt her down. He'll know just what to do. Our kind just doesn't like wolves. Panthers are much more superior to those fucking animals any day."

He looked at Jane when she stood up and took his pen from his hand. She wrote something on another sheet of paper and handed it to him. Then she left the office. Thad was almost afraid to read it, but when he did, he felt a chill run down his spine that made the hair on the back of his neck dance.

"I'll take care of him. Vampires are much more superior to panthers any day." Thad let Morton go on and on. He wasn't sure if it was because everything had gotten so surreal or that he wasn't sure what to do now. Thad thought it was a good case of both, and when Morton said Jane was at his door, he had the overwhelming urge to tell him good luck. But he hung up the phone and waited.

Jane returned an hour later, and she simply went to her desk. He didn't ask her, though he wanted to know what had happened in his foreman's office. When she came into his office again and sat across from him, he tried his best not to notice the drop of blood on her blouse. It might have been there this morning, he kept telling himself.

"There's a major front moving through Ohio right now, and will be for the next several hours. I have you booked to Chicago, the closest I could get you, and have arranged for you to have an SUV there for you to drive the rest of the way." She handed him a file, and he took it from her without speaking. "There are driving instructions in there, as well as hotels that you can…. Are you all right? You look like you're going to freak out."

"I am. I don't…you're a vampire." It wasn't a question, but she answered him with a nod. "And Morton was a panther. Diamond and her family are wolves, and there is more of your kind on my staff?"

"Yes. I would say about half your management staff is, and more of your floor staff. We, well most of us, thought you were aware of us but had some sort of don't ask don't tell kind of thing going on." She leaned back and watched him carefully as she continued. "You're not mated with Diamond, are you? The reason I say that is because while I can smell her on you, you don't actually have her scent."

"Sex you mean?" She nodded. "No, we didn't have sex. I didn't…I had no idea what she was or you were, for that matter. Sapphire knew, she and Blair told me when they explained to me what they were. Not who was what, but that I had a few of you on my staff. I think…fuck, I fucking lost it and said some things that I'm sure I didn't mean."

"Doubtful. You say what you mean and stick to it." She stretched out her legs in front of her and smiled. He could see her fangs now, and he was sure it was because she was letting him.

"What did you do to Morton?" She shook her head, and he decided that he really didn't want to know. "I don't think they're going to let me go back, and I'm pretty sure that something happened to Diamond or one of the others."

"I can find out. You won't ask me how I find out, but I can find out." He nodded as she stood up and moved to the door.

"I really screwed this up with her. I'm not saying that I'll want her as my mate, but I didn't want anything to happen to her." Jane turned to stare at him, and he could see fear there. "What is it? What do you already know?"

"She's your mate. And weres bond for life. But if you don't take her, then did...did they tell you what would happen now that she's taken a part of you in her? I'm assuming that's what happened. Diamond somehow has taken your blood?"

"I was hurt in that car accident and she healed me." Thad stood up to pace as he tried to think. "She licked it and I healed. Blair said she took my blood and we have a bond."

"She's hurt. Badly, I would say, by the way you fell over." He stopped packing to wait for her to explain. "You have a connection, and I'm not one hundred percent sure why you felt her pain without mating, but you did. She's hurt."

"And what happens if I don't take her as my mate? You started to tell me, what is it?" Her phone started to ring, but neither of them moved to answer it. He waited, knowing that whatever it was, it was going to be bad.

"She'll turn rogue and will need to be put down if it gets bad enough. All of us have the potential to turn at some point in our lives. Boredom mostly. But only because we have no one to share our lives with, to help us, and be there for us or, sadly, the loss of our mates. If we can't find a way to overcome it, we...we start to turn bad, kill for fun and pleasure. Most vampires meet the sun when their mates die, others like me try to cope."

"You lost your mate?" Jane nodded again. "Was he human? Did you have a human as your mate?"

"Yes, and she was the light of my life, and all I wanted to live for. But before she died, she told me that I was to live on for her, do things that she was no longer able to do." Jane shrugged. "So I have to the best of my ability. For the past four hundred years I've been alone, and every day I wake to wonder if it wouldn't be easier to just simply let myself go. But as a half-vamp, I don't have a lot of options to end my life without trusting someone to do it for me, and quickly."

He sat on the conference table because it was the closest thing to him without falling to the floor. Jane stood there and watched him for several seconds before she turned and left his office, closing the door softly behind her. Thad was still sitting there when she returned a few minutes later.

"Diamond has been shot. And worse yet, with a silver bullet. Someone named Ruby removed it, but she won't shift." He waited for her to continue. "If she doesn't shift to remove the poison from her system, she'll die. Not quickly, either, with the silver removed. I'm surprised her alpha hasn't pulled her wolf."

"Blair. He told me he was alpha and that he ruled...how would he pull her wolf?" She handed him a thick book, and he looked at the cover. It was old and leather bound. It had a circle of wolves chasing one another, and in the center of the circle was a single word. *Lupine.*

"That was given to me by someone a very long time ago. When I first smelled the wolves after you came back, I had thought that you'd found a woman and had no idea what you'd...never mind. I brought it to work in the event you had known what you smelled like. Then I met the Hensons and knew. Again, I thought you'd ask for more information on them, but you didn't." She took the book back and searched through the pages until she found what she was looking for. Thad took it back from her and read the title. "Human and Wolf Mating Rituals"

"I would read that first since you're well beyond anything previous in the book." She handed him his coat as she continued. "Your car is downstairs, and the plane is ready to go. If you have any questions, just call me. I don't sleep."

Thad was in the limo when he realized that he had nothing to wear once he got there, and started to ask the driver when his phone signaled he had a message. Opening the file, he laughed at the message from Jane.

"Clothes are easy to buy, so get something less stiff and something more befitting a man, not a billionaire. I have made arrangements with Blair's office to set up an appointment, but since he is working from home for now, you'll have to see him there. Don't fuck this up. If you do, I'll drain you. Have a good day."

"Christ," he thought out loud. He was headed to Ohio to see to a woman who may or may not eat him for dinner, to talk to a man who would most assuredly kill him if he didn't have answers, and literally into a den of wolves who had been hurt by him. Yeah, this was going to go well.

Chapter 6

Blair was sitting at his desk when the door opened. He'd been trying to concentrate on business, but his heart just wasn't in it. He looked up at Annabelle when she came fully into the room.

"You have a visitor. Thad Galloway is here. I put him in the living room." Blair started to tell her to get him the hell out, but she raised her hand up to continue. "He looks like you do."

"And what is that?" Blair knew what he looked like. Sapphire had told him this morning that she was glad he wasn't at his office. He would scare most of his staff and probably have them all quit if he barked at them like he was her.

"Like you've lost something very dear to you." She stood up and moved to the door but turned to speak again. "He asked me about Diamond. I told him that she was…coping. I wanted to tell him that she's dying, but I can't say that to anyone."

Blair had never hated anyone as much as he did Thad. The man had sent a fucking gun there to keep him in line, and now he was sitting in the house as if nothing had happened. Blair didn't want to see him, not now, not ever, but he knew that if he threw him out of the house he'd just find Diamond other ways. Blair looked up at the ceiling, thinking of the woman who was up there and how much he loved her.

Thad knocked on the open door, and Blair was shocked at how badly he did look. And if he looked like that, he was glad now that he'd not left the house. Christ, the man looked like he'd been shot.

"I've been trying to get here for five days. If it wasn't the weather, it was the car I rented. Then I got a bout of food poisoning and was…it doesn't matter. I've come to see Diamond please. I'd like to talk to her."

"She won't see you. Not just you, but none of us. She's in her room." Blair wanted to beg him to take her as his mate, but because of the promises he'd made Diamond, he couldn't do anything like that. "I'd very much like it if you got the hell out of my life. I don't want you here."

"According to what I've read, you can pull her wolf to make her shift. Why haven't you done that?" Blair was shocked that Thad had bothered to find out any information on them, but he continued before Blair could say anything. "There have been incidents where the she-wolf is strong enough to resist the alpha, but not if she's hurt badly. Also, it says that you can heal her if she won't do it herself."

"She's been shot, did you know that? And by one of your men you sent out here to take care of us. Did you know that he had everything all written out and what to do to harm this family?" Blair was shaking his head at him. "You're saying you didn't mean for him to shoot us in cold blood?"

"I didn't send him out here." Blair sat back in his chair as Thad continued. "I didn't know until…when she was hurt, so was I. Jane told me that it wasn't possible since we didn't mate, but I felt her shot in the belly."

Blair had to think, but his thoughts weren't going in any direction that made sense to him. Then something occurred to him. It had been Morton. He didn't know why he knew it, but he looked at Thad and asked him.

"Morton sent them out here to stop this deal from happening, didn't he?" Thad nodded. "Why? Does he think that we were going to…I don't know, roll over and let you fuck us up over this?"

"I don't know what he thought, and as of almost a week ago, he's dead." Blair started to ask what happened when Thad stood, pacing. "She wouldn't tell me what she did, and I really didn't want to know. Jane, I mean. Did you know she was a vampire? I didn't. Apparently, more than half the people working for me are some sort of paranormal. But she went to his office, and no one has heard or seen him since. She simply told me to hire someone else."

Blair knew she was a vampire, not a full blooded one but close enough. He also knew that she was a great deal older than she looked. Maybe as much as five hundred years more than she looked. But he let Thad pace and mumble while he reached for Sapphire.

"Thad is here in my office, and he's had a great shock. He's also more bonded with Diamond than we'd thought. He felt her pain when she was hurt." Blair knew his wife was at her office and wondered for a second if she was getting any work done either.

"Are you going to let him see her? I don't know if I would or not. She needs something to pull her out of this even if she were to shift to kill him." Blair laughed a little, and Thad stared at him before continuing on his trek across his carpet. *"I'd let her see him, I think. Just to see if she has any feelings for him."*

"Do you think she does?" He'd tried talking to her several times over the past week, but all she'd done was tell him to go away. Then yesterday she'd told him that if they all didn't stop bothering her, she'd go to New York now and not contact them at all. If she did that, he knew she'd let herself go and die without anyone knowing until it was too late.

"I think if she didn't have feelings for him, she'd have shifted and been on her way to recovering by now. And if it's simply hatred and she kills him, well, I can live with that too."

Blair watched Thad pace, and when he finally sat down, he put a book on his desk. Every part of him froze when he saw the title and he looked up at the man to ask him where the hell he'd gotten it when he answered his unspoken question.

"Jane said that someone gave it to her years and years ago. I didn't ask her where, but she told me to read it. When I was hospitalized, I had to do something since I didn't have the strength to do much else, so I read it. From cover to cover, making notes on some of the things I didn't understand." He pulled out a tattered notebook and opened it. "Like this part about changing your mate to a wolf. It says that she has to cause me a mortal wound. Why?"

"So that her essences enter your body quickly. Sometimes the human dies when this happens, but for the most part, in a few days to a week the human lives because he's been changed to wolf." Blair picked up the book with trembling hands. "Do you know what this book could do for my kind if it were to fall into the wrong hands?"

"They would hunt you down and kill you all. I would imagine that over the years someone had gotten this book. There's a whole section at the end of it that's been added by hand. They told of the massacre in which thousands of your kind were killed and a great many humans that they thought werewolf just to get rid of you." Thad looked at his notes. "I would never say a word to anyone, and I want you to have the book. Jane said I was to do with it what I wanted. You are the only person I trust with it."

Blair felt oddly honored and terrified. To have such a book was an honor. Also to have it was scary. The book in the wrong hands could do so much more than what Thad thought it could. It would quite literally end the existence of all weres everywhere.

"She's dying." Thad looked up at him when he spoke. "She won't shift and because of a promise I made her last summer, I can't command her to do anything like this. At the time I thought it was because she didn't care for going to the pack meetings and she didn't want to have to shift because of what happened to her before with her other pack. But she sort of has me at a hold. No matter how much I command her to shift, she won't. I think she wants to die."

"Because of me." Blair didn't answer him. He wasn't sure he could tell him anything other than he was correct. "Can I make her shift?"

"No. Well, that's not true, you more than likely could, but it would be...it would require you pissing her off so badly that her wolf would take her." Blair started to tell him it was dangerous but he stood up and nodded.

"Is she in her room?" Blair nodded and watched the man walk away. He wanted to go after him and tell him to not do this, but he had nothing invested in the man and everything in the woman. Diamond was a very big part of this family, as were all the others, and her being this way, dying and not really caring, he was willing to let him be hurt instead of her. And right now, he was their only hope of saving her.

~~~

Diamond moved slowly from the bathroom to the bed. She wanted to make it up, the sheets needed changing too, but she didn't have the energy, and even if she did, she wasn't sure she'd do it anyway. The knock at her door had her groaning. Why didn't they simply leave her alone? When it opened, she stared at Thad for a long time before he moved into the room completely and closed the door behind him.

"What are you doing here? I think you should leave." She felt her wolf stir a little. "Now, before you piss me off."

"You look like shit." Her entire body felt the hit of embarrassment when he said that. "Not only that, but you smell. What the hell have you been doing up here, hibernating? I'm opening a window and airing this place out."

"You'll do no such thing. I said for you to get out, now." The cool breeze from the window took her breath away. And the scents from the now open window made her wolf claw at her. Thad stood near the window and looked out over the yard. Diamond would have closed it again but he wasn't moving.

"You're going to die up here, and no one will be the wiser unless you let out some of the stench in here. They'll simply think you've still not bathed." Thad turned to look at her as he continued. "Right now I'd very much like to pick you up and toss you in the shower myself, but I don't want to reek of you."

Her wolf stirred against her skin, hard and hot. When Thad took a step back from her, she knew he'd felt it too. Diamond tried her best to calm her, but she wasn't having it. She wanted to hurt the man in front of them.

"You should leave." Thad shook his head and crossed his arms over his chest, looking for all the world like he was ready to do battle with her. "You are pissing off my wolf, and she wants to hurt you."

"You think I care? I don't. I'm not afraid of you. Other than you making me sick to my stomach. Did you really think that sitting up here in this room was going to endear you to anyone? All you've done is make people feel sorry for you. Big bad Diamond Erickson is so messed up from some guy that she's willing to let herself die over him." He snorted. "I guess you're not half the woman they think you are. At least I will know the truth."

Her wolf snarled at her and took her. Pain radiated from her entire body as fur replaced skin; bones took another shape and size under her skin and made her drop to her hands. Claws sprouted from her fingers so that she looked as if she had a monster growing from her. When she felt her wolf tear at her face, elongating her chin until she had a muzzle, teeth grew along her newly formed jaw until she knew that when she bit at something she'd tear and mash, bringing blood down her throat to drink from. Diamond blinked several times, waiting for her eyes to adjust before she looked at Thad.

"You should know that I didn't mean anything I said to you. Before or now. I was a fool. But Blair told me that you needed to shift and this was the only way." She moved closer to him and he didn't run like her wolf wanted him to but stood very still. "I was more than a fool, Diamond, I was...I should have been...I'm not sure what I could have said or done that would have made things better between us."

You don't want me. He looked shocked at her, and she knew that he'd heard her. *You made me feel like I was worthless, less than human. You made me feel worse than Jeffery ever did. She wants to kill you right now.*

"I don't know who that is but I'm assuming he's the guy that hurt you into not wanting to shift at pack meetings." Thad sat down on the chair and she could smell his weakness. "I know that you'll never forgive me, and I can understand that. I was a bastard and a—"

What's wrong with you? Diamond moved closer to him but not close enough that she could touch him. *You smell like...you're sick. What's happened to you?*

"I'm fine." She snarled at him, and he leaned away from her when she got closer. "I was sick for a few days. I'm better now."

You're not. You smell like you're still very sick and should be in a hospital. He didn't move, but she did until she could put her nose on his bare arm. You come in here acting like you can take on the world and...what if I had attacked you? How the hell would you have defended yourself against me?

Then it occurred to her that he didn't care if she killed him or not. When she whimpered at him, he put his hand on her head and rubbed against her fur. Leaning into him, she let him continue touching her; the wolf in her was happy with him all of a sudden.

"I'm going to have to go soon. I'm flying out tonight." Thad started to stand but fell back in the chair. "I'm glad that you're going to be well from now on. I'm not sure why Blair let me in the house, but I guess he figured that having me dead and you alive was a better tradeoff for all of you. And I'm not going to fight the...did you know Jane was a vampire?"

He was burning up, and she could feel his heat. Diamond had to shift back to help him, but was afraid to leave him. She reached for Blair. He would help her.

Come to my room quickly. Thad is sick and I'm worried about him. Diamond heard him running to her and when the door burst open, he was standing there. *He's ill. He came in here to piss me off and you let him, knowing he was this sick.*

Blair picked him up and put him on her bed. She didn't care right now where he was so long as he was put somewhere she could help him. Diamond went to the bathroom and shifted. This time it was much easier on her, and quicker. She pulled on the first things she could find and went back to her room. Blair was taking off his pants, having already pulled off his shoes and socks.

"He's burning up." Blair nodded at her. "I need you to find my bag please, the one that I have down in the kitchen."

While he was gone, Diamond tore Thad's shirt and realized how much weight he'd lost...a great deal more than what was healthy. When Blair returned, she pulled out what she could and dumped the rest on the floor. Setting him up with an IV turned out to be harder than she'd thought it would be because she was shaking so hard. When a hand lay across her hand, she looked up at her grandmother.

"Take a deep breath and steady yourself. The way you're going right now, you're going to harm him more than help him. Breathe, Diamond, he needs you." Nodding, Diamond closed her eyes and listened to her grandmother's soothing voice. "That's it, just in and out like you know how to do."

As calmness settled over her, Diamond looked down at his arm. The veins were sunken and his skin dry. He'd been ill for more than a day, she'd bet, and looked at Blair when he came into the room. She asked him what he knew.

"He said he had food poisoning and that he'd been in the hospital. He didn't say how long, but I would think for a few days." Blair handed her a strip of tape before she'd asked for it. "I think he looks worse now than when he was in my office."

"I think him pissing me off took its toll on him. I didn't even realize how sick he was until he pissed me off." She glanced up at Blair. "You told him to do that knowing how sick he was? What if I had hurt him or, worse yet, killed him?"

"You're right. It was a chance I was willing to take to get you better. I was also hoping that as your mate you'd not be able to harm him." Blair picked up her things as she hung an IV bag from her canopy as he continued. "He gave me a book."

"Good for you. Now will you please get out? I have things to take care of in here and you're too much male for my wolf. She wants to hurt you right now for harming what she thinks of as hers."

"And what do you think of him?" Diamond didn't answer him because she wasn't sure what she thought. The man had rejected her, and not only that but had shamed her as well. "Diamond?"

"He's going to get better. Then I'm sending him on his way. Thad Galloway no more wants me than I do him." Lie, her wolf snarled at her. "Now please see if you can get some supplies from your clinic for me. I'll need whatever you can put your hands on in the form of antibiotics for a human."

He nodded and left her sitting on the edge of the bed. Diamond looked down at Thad and wondered if he'd die. It was just about what she deserved for taking on a human mate. When Thad started to toss and turn, she moved over him, pressing him down with her body, and he stilled.

Every time she started to move off the bed, he'd moan and start to toss off the covers. Diamond finally gave up and lay down beside him, holding him in her arms throughout the night. And just as the sun was blazing over the room, Thad's fever broke and she fell asleep, holding him to her.

Chapter 7

Thad woke feeling heavy and hot. He tried to move away from the source of heat, but every time he was inches away, he'd be pulled back quickly and held tighter. Using what very little strength he had, he looked down at the inferno in his arms.

Diamond was lying with her head over his chest and both her arms wrapped tightly around him. Even her leg was over his, her weight making it so that he couldn't move even if he wanted to. She turned her head over so that he could see her face when she spoke.

"Shhhh, you'll be fine in a few hours. Just rest, I've got you." When her leg moved up his thigh and over his groin, his cock jerked hard, and that's when he realized he was naked.

"Diamond, you have to move off me. I don't have the energy to take you right now." She moaned again and then nipped at his nipple. Blair thought he was going to explode when he felt her warm breath over him. "Baby, you're making me hard as stone and as needy as hell."

A burst of giggles had him shifted on the bed so that she was over him rather than beside him. When she sat up slightly, he could see she was still a little asleep and he was not only awake right now but fully aroused and in pain. Dawning of what was going on came to her quickly.

"You're awake." He nodded and rocked upward. "You should be asleep for a few more days. I was going to leave you here after I took a nap."

"I don't want you to leave me just yet." He pulled her up higher over his body and moved again into her heat. "Did you take off my clothes?"

"You were sweating and had soaked them through." She moved over him now so that her legs were on both sides of him and her hands on his chest. "You seem to be much better now. Perhaps I should leave you to rest."

Grabbing her hips, he held her over him and rocked up again. There was no way he was going to willingly let her get out of the bed. Running his hands up her back and just under her tee–shirt, he touched warm, almost hot skin. This time he moaned.

"No." When she rolled her hips over him, he rolled her to her back with him cradled between her legs. "Do you have any idea what I want to do to you right now? I want to show you so much. But all I can think of is drinking from you, then pounding deep inside of you."

"I don't think you have the energy for that just yet." All Thad could think about was that she'd not told him no. He lifted slightly from her body and lifted her shirt. He nearly whimpered when he realized that she had no bra on and he could taste her as long as he wanted. Leaning down to her pert nipple, he bit her just enough for a small pain but nothing like he wanted to do.

His body was weak, yes, but he was gaining strength by leaps and bounds now. When she curled her fingers into his hair, he nipped harder on her nipple and felt her rock up into him. He had to taste her.

The journey down her torso was amazing. There were so many places to bite her and to lick her that he nearly forgot where he'd been headed. By the time he got to her navel, he was ready to beg her to ride him but her scent, now that he was close enough to smell her, was driving him insane. Sitting up between her legs, he looked down at what she was wearing.

A pair of his boxer briefs, if he wasn't mistaken. They were his favorites too. Dark blue silk stuck to her skin where her pussy was because she was so wet. Sliding his hand up the leg of them, he watched her face for any signs she wasn't ready for him.

"You're very wet for me." Diamond nodded. "I'd love to punish you for not asking permission from me to wear them, but right now all I can think of is that you're making it very easy for me to get what I want."

"What do you want?" He had a feeling she was asking more than what he wanted right now but wanted to play before she was mad again. Because Thad just realized he was very close to wanting it all.

"I want to do all kinds of things to you. Do you know what I mean when I say I'm a player?" She shook her head and he danced his fingers up near the apex of her thighs and stopped. "I'm a Dom, a dominant over you sexually. I want you to submit to me in all things."

"You want to hurt me." He heard the breathlessness of her voice and was willing to bet she wanted this too. "I don't like pain."

"You will. From me." Thad slid his fingers into her pussy as he continued to watch her face. "I will reward you greatly if you do what I say. Right now all I can think about is letting you come as much as you want so I can have my fill, but I won't let you do that very often. I want you to obey me."

"You don't want me. You said...you called me a thing." Diamond moved her hips in a way that he was no longer deep inside of her but just at her clit. If she moved again, he'd have to start again and he wasn't ready for that.

He pinched her clit hard. When she cried out, he did it again and again until she was riding his fingers rather than pulling away. Thad wanted to prove to her that she was his and leaned over her, still holding her clit and bit her nipple.

"Come for me now, slave." Her body bowed up, and she grabbed his arms as she screamed out her release. It was violent in its intensity and he loved every minute of it. When he commanded her to come again, she dug her nails deep into his forearms as she rode his fingers like he wanted her to ride his mouth. Moving down her body, he tore his boxers from her and dove into her wet heat.

Christ, she tasted better than she smelled. Thad slid his fingers into her and was rewarded with copious amounts of cream that he had a hard time keeping up with. He lapped hard at her pussy, drinking as much as he could before he slid another finger deep and scissored them to stretch her for him.

Thad knew he was close. Reaching down to stroke his cock, he realized that he had no protection for her and had a sudden thought of her large with his child. Never had thoughts of anyone having his baby occurred to him until that moment. Then he remembered what the book had said about her having to be in heat. Thad wanted her to be in heat now so he could fill her with his child. Biting her clit again and sucking hard, she came in his mouth and he realized how much more he wanted.

Sitting up, he reluctantly left her body. Diamond moaned at him, and he wanted to go back and give her what she wanted. She sat up and looked at him as he stroked his thick, hard cock.

"Spread your legs wider for me. I want to watch your pretty pussy ready for me." She opened her legs wider, and he pinched her thigh. "When I tell you to do something, I need you to repeat it back to me and say 'Yes, master.'" She looked angry, and he was sure he was going to have to tell her again when she finally spoke.

"I'll spread wide for you as you wish, master." He nearly came all over her when she dropped her eyes. Then she looked up at him and he was suddenly afraid. "If you fuck me now it will be as mates. There will be no way you can leave me now or I you. Is that what you want?"

He did. He had an idea that they were well beyond that anyway, but she wanted him to say it. It would be the last time he would allow her to ask him questions like this so long as they were in the bedroom. Thad remembered the part in the book about mates bonding and tried to remember the wording of it. He smiled when he remembered as he moved his cock at her entrance.

"You're my mate in all things. I take unto me all that you are and give you all that I am. I will protect you with my life, honor you in all things, and respect you more than any being could. I take you as my mate." Thad moved his cock into her slowly with each sentence. By the time he was seated as far as he could go, she had wrapped her legs around him and held him to her.

"You must bite me when we come. Break skin and…. Oh Christ, yes that feels so good." He moved again, this time harder and deeper. "When we come, please mark me. Bite me, Thad, please."

He'd never been a biter much, but he found he wanted to bite her. Sweat poured down his spine as he held himself still inside of her. He wanted her to look at him, but he wouldn't tell her. It was her job to ask him what he wanted.

When she raised her eyes to look at him, he kissed her hard, putting all his pent-up sexual need into it. Diamond gave as well as she got, and he nearly cried out when she bit his lower lip and then suckled it into her warm mouth.

"Come." Her body responded to his command like he'd hoped. Better than he hoped if he was honest. When she licked along his throat to his shoulder, he did the same to her, following the same path until he felt her nip at his muscle there. When she whispered through his mind, he started moving in and out of her until she was taking him as deep as he could go.

I'm so close right now that when you sink your teeth into me and draw on my blood, I'm going to come like I've never come before. He nipped none too gently at her shoulder as she continued. *Bite me and drink from me. I want to feel you come now.*

Thad's climax exploded over him, making him not just see stars but to feel them detonate over every part of him as he sank his teeth into her flesh. The moment her blood touched his tongue, he tore his mouth from her and threw back his head. This climax made him see pinpoints of light everywhere as his body seemed to explode another release out of him.

Diamond pulled him to her and jerked his head back. He felt her tongue again as it moved down his throat to his shoulder. When she bit him, Thad came again, this one so hard and fast that it made his vision blur and his mind scream for him to hang on. His last thoughts as he fell atop her were that he was never going to survive sleeping with her.

~~~

Diamond was sitting in the kitchen having a cup of tea when Sapphire walked in. She didn't speak to her until she had her own cup and a piece of toast. The two of them had always been very close, but she had a feeling that she was mad at her for some reason.

"You were willing to leave us all behind instead of doing the right thing." Diamond nodded but didn't look at her. "Do you have any idea how worried you made all of us because you were too selfish to let us help you?"

"I know what I was doing and the fact that you let me do it was more appreciated than I can ever tell you." Sapphire snorted, and Diamond looked up at her. "I think I killed him."

Sapphire stared at her for several seconds before she threw back her head and laughed. It sounded so good that Diamond joined her. When Sapphire reached for her hand, Diamond curled her into hers and held it tightly.

"Don't do that again, please. I don't know what I would do without you." Diamond nodded and felt Thad stir in her bed and looked up at the ceiling. "You and him have mated and bonded then, I take it?"

"We have. I'm not sure whether or not we'll make it, but for now we're going okay." Diamond didn't mention the things he said in his sleep, because she wasn't sure what they had meant. "He was really sick when he came here. I think he was willing to die in order to make me shift."

"Blair said the same thing after he helped you get him into bed. He also said you were going to take away that stupid promise you made him give you. I really wish you would. It would have been so much easier if you hadn't made him hold back." Diamond didn't say anything. She wasn't going to give him back the promise. If this thing with Thad didn't work out, she wanted an option. And the less her sister knew the better about that.

"He's up." They both heard the water through the pipes, and Diamond went to the refrigerator. Her grandmother wasn't home, having gone to the grocery store, so she decided to make him something to eat. She started to pull out the bacon and other breakfast items, knowing that Thad was going to be starved when he came down. She flushed when she thought of him in her bed and the things he'd done to her. Also, she wanted to look up some things on the computer about this Dom/sub thing he'd told her about. Sapphire pulled out the flour to make what Diamond hoped was biscuits. By the time Blair came into the kitchen they were well on their way to having everything ready. Thad walked in a few minutes later.

"Hello." He pulled her into his arms and kissed her. She was wrapping her arms around his neck and pulling him closer to her when she heard someone clear their throat. Diamond looked at Blair.

"For as much as it makes me happy that you've found your mate and all, Sapphire and I have work to do." Blair moved to the newly installed coffee machine and started it up as he continued. "I'm assuming you're going back now, Thad. Can't say that I'll be sad to see you go, but we need to figure out what do to with your relationship with my sister."

"I'm not leaving." Everyone turned to look at Thad. "I may have to go back for a few days now and then, but I'm not leaving her, nor will I take her from her family. I have a feeling it would never work anyway."

He took the platter of bacon and ham from her and put it on the table. Thad smiled at her as he gave her a quick kiss on the mouth and sat down. No one moved as Thad continued.

"I was wrong. On a great many levels, but saying the things I did hurt you all, and I'm profoundly sorry for that." He got up and shoved her in a chair before getting her cup of tea and setting it beside her plate. "I don't know how this will work out, but I'd very much like to live here until we can find a place of our own. There are a great many houses around the area that are—"

"You're not living here." Blair flushed and lowered his voice as he continued. "I mean you can visit, but I don't think it will work out with you living here and us being on opposite side of things with this vegetable tray."

"Have you sold the idea yet?" Blair looked at Sapphire, then back at Thad before he shook his head. "Good. I would very much like to go back to the drawing board with this. I don't mean your end, but on my end. I want to start a production company here that would mass produce the containers as well as the fluid containers that Sapphire and I talked about before."

"You think that just because you saved Diamond that you can simply waltz right back in here as if nothing happened?" Blair sat down and slammed his cup on the table, sloshing coffee everywhere as he continued. "It doesn't work that way, buddy. I have my reputation to uphold, as well as Sapphire. You can't be seriously thinking we'd want to work with—"

"How many people would you hire for startup?" Blair huffed at Sapphire when she cut him off. "Think about it for a minute. Where will we be if he decides to move to Texas and takes my sister with him? Or better yet, what will happen to the others of our pack if something doesn't happen soon with the job situation here?"

"I can't go to Texas." Everyone looked at her. "I'm not sure we'll be able to make this thing between us work out, but I'm not moving again. I don't want to.... What if things don't work out between us? Then I'm stuck all the way across the United States and no one to help me come back."

"You're not going to have to worry about this between us. I realize what we did yesterday was big, huge really, and I'm not going to let you get away from me again. I'll make this work." She was shaking her head at him when he continued. "We'll make this work. And as soon as possible I want to be changed...converted, I think they called it."

She sat there playing with her food as the rest of them talked. Argued really, but she didn't listen in. He wanted to make this work, and she was afraid he would too. Diamond didn't want a mate that would hurt her when he was pissed off, nor did she want one that thought he could dominate her either. When his hand touched her thigh, she stilled.

We need to find us a home so that when you make me scream out my climax, I don't have to worry about others hearing me. Diamond felt her body heat at his words. *I've also made a few calls before coming down here. There are two bondage shops, as well as a club here in town. I'd very much like to take you there tonight. I want you to enjoy my dominating you as much as I do. I want you to keep an open mind and let me show you what pleasures there are for us. Can you do that for me?*

And if I don't like it, will you drop me again like I'm a diseased animal? The words were out before she could stop them, and when his hand squeezed her thigh, she looked at him as the others stepped out of the kitchen. She wondered how they knew but right now didn't care.

I won't do that to you ever again. I swear to you. But if you don't like what we do in the bedroom, I'll understand, but I'm betting you will. Very much so. Thad turned in his seat and took both her hands and spoke aloud to her. "You came hard last night because you let me dominate you. If you don't want this lifestyle, we can make love like other couples. But once you let me show you, you'll see."

Would she? Did she really want to? He leaned in and took her mouth for a slow and very thorough kiss. When he cupped the back of her head and pulled her closer, she was suddenly sitting over him on his lap. He never stopped kissing her as he lifted her tee-shirt up and cupped her breast. Moisture pooled between her thighs, and she tried to squirm around so that he wouldn't smell her.

"Don't do that." His hand between her legs had her rolling her hips up to meet him. "I'd very much like to lay you over this table and eat you."

"They'll hear us." Diamond didn't recognize her own voice as he continued to torment her nipple through her bra. When he leaned her back and she touched the table, he lifted her bra up and took her breast into his mouth, and she knew she was going to come like this.

"Don't even think about it. If you come now, I'll take you to our bedroom and paddle your ass hard. When you come, it will be because I say you can." Diamond was nodding even before he finished. When he pinched her breast hard, she looked up at him and realized what he wanted.

"I'll not come until you say I can or you'll take me up and paddle my ass. Master." He nodded at her and went back to her breast. The more he nibbled on her nipple the harder she wanted to say fuck it and come anyway. But the thought of disappointing him was right there, and she found she didn't want to do that either.

When he lifted his head from her, she wanted to beg him for relief, but he only helped her stand and held her hand when she wobbled slightly. Sitting back in her chair, she tried to be upset with him but found she only felt proud of herself.

"What are your plans for the rest of the day?" She tried to think if this was part of his plan when he lifted her chin up and looked at her. "Sex is the only time I'll ever try to control you. I will want you to be willing to have sex with me anywhere I want, but for now we'll work on a home for us. Once we are in the bedroom, I'm your master, otherwise we're just a couple trying to make things work."

"Why?" He looked at her strangely. "Why do you want us to be a couple now when a week ago you were disgusted with me…with what I am? The sex with you is great, but not worth you changing your mind in a few months when I've fallen in love with you."

"Because for the first time in my life I want someone to fall in love with me. And I want that to be you. I'm not saying I love you now, but I do care for you. A great deal, as a matter of fact." He took her hand into his. "I've said this to you before, but I want you to hear it over and over until you believe me. I'm sorry for what I did to you. Sorrier than I've ever been for anything in my life. I want you to forgive me because you believe me, and I know that that's a long way in coming. If ever."

Chapter 8

Ward Galloway looked around the plane, trying to figure out why he'd been sitting in coach instead of in first class. There were empty seats as far as he could see, but the stewardess told him his ticket wasn't upgradable and for him to please stay in his seat. He supposed he shouldn't have irritated her so much and he might have been able to convince her that he was first-class material.

"Would you like something to drink, sir?" Ward looked up at the women who had been standoffish to him earlier. "We have beverages as well as a few snacks."

"I'd like a bourbon and coke please." He waited for her to tell him no, but she only quoted him a price. "For a bourbon and coke? You've got to be kidding me. Who pays that much for a drink on a goddamned plane?"

"Sir, I'm going to have to ask you to lower your voice and to keep your language cleaner. There are children on this flight that wouldn't like to hear that from someone they don't know." In other words, she was telling him that she didn't believe that the kids hadn't heard it before, just not from him. "Now, would you like the drink or not?"

Testy and a bit on the short side, her voice could have chilled the bowels of hell. Ward shook his head but decided for as much trouble as they were giving him on this damned flight he'd get what he had coming to him.

"What do you charge for a regular soft drink? And I don't mean a little tiny glass, but the whole can." Ward smiled at her and didn't even bother trying to charm her any longer. He was right, and she fucking well knew it.

"I can't leave you the can, sir, because in the event of turbulence we don't want the can to be bouncing around hitting someone." She started to move on, but he grabbed her arm. He realized his mistake the moment she turned back to him.

It was over almost before it started. The stewardess by day and sumo wrestler by night had him flipped out of his seat and on the floor before he could say a word. Then when she banged his head against the hard cart she'd been pushing up and down the aisle, Ward knew all sorts of pain. She was going to kill him and throw him from the plane. He just knew it.

When one of the pilots came back and "helped" her pick him up, dropping him three times and banging him against whatever he could, Ward was put in a seat in the very back of the plane and the big man sat next to him. This was not going to be a good flight after all, he thought.

"You should know better than to touch anyone without permission." The man popped him in the face with his elbow as he started to stand. "Oh, sorry about that."

Ward didn't for a second believe he was the least bit sorry, but said nothing. He had a feeling if he opened his mouth for any reason, there would be a fist in it and he'd be bleeding from more than just his lip. When he was left alone, he waited for the cart to make its way toward him because he wanted some ice. The stewardess just went right by him without a word, and he turned to yell at her when the man returned to stand next to him again.

"Problem?" Ward shook his head at him. "Good. See that there isn't from now on or so help me I'll make sure you end up on a plane going in a place that is best not visited by pansy-assed pricks like you." Ward decided that he was going to have a word with Morton when he saw him next for booking him on a plane with a bunch of assholes.

Ward had heard from his friend Morton eight days ago. He'd told him to come to Texas and see what his brother was up to. Ward hadn't heard from Thad in almost ten years, so really hadn't cared all that much about him or what he was up to, much less enough to travel all the way across the United States to check it out. But Morton had insisted that Thad had had a change of heart and thought it would be great if he came out and surprised him.

Fat chance of that happening. But the ticket had shown up the next afternoon and a quick call to Morton had confirmed that Thad had not only sent it but had insisted that he come for a long visit. He had his suspicions but didn't say them to Morton. Thad and he had never gotten along. But Ward had hopped on the plane the next morning and now here he was flying across the States to see his long-lost brother. But now he couldn't get in touch with Morton.

Calling his office had given him no information, and when he'd called his house, there was someone there who started asking questions almost as soon as he answered. The man had wanted his name and address and why he was calling, but Ward had hung up. Something about his tone made him think that something had happened to Morton, and it wasn't good.

Thad had made him leave his house all those years ago because he'd caught him doing something that had offended him. Ward didn't understand then and certainly didn't understand any better now why Thad had such a problem with what he'd been doing. It wasn't as if he didn't have all kinds of money.

"You'll not get another dime from me. Not now and not ever. I'm finished with you." Thad had had him cuffed to the chair in the big conference room in the Galloway building like he was nothing to him. "And as for all the money you took, you'll pay it back or I'll press charges."

"Are you fucking kidding me? Where the hell would I get that kind of money? And if you think I'm selling my stuff, you're nutty as a fruit fly." Ward had jerked on the cuffs around his wrists. "Get these things off me. You can't treat me this way. I'm a Galloway."

No one had moved to release him and he jerked on them again. Thad asked the others to step out; three men that had guns at their waist as well as dark glasses that hid whatever they were thinking about what was going on.

"As of this morning, everything in your apartment has been removed. That includes the clothing you had there and all the jewelry you purchased with my money." Ward tried to lunge at his brother but only managed to hurt himself and have Thad laugh at him. "You were caught, why don't you admit it?"

"Caught at what? Taking a little off the top?" Ward hadn't waited for his brother to answer because he really didn't care what he'd had to say. "You make more money in one week than most people make in a lifetime. What the hell do you care if I take a few extra bucks? You're supposed to care for me. I'm your little brother. Doesn't the Galloway name mean shit to you?"

"It was nearly five million dollars over an eight month period, and you're lucky that I don't have you up on charges." Thad had stood and towered over him as he looked down at him in more ways than one. "You'll be escorted out of this building and put onto the streets. The money you have in your pockets is all you'll ever see from me again. The credit cards are now closed, as are the bank accounts and all other privileges that you seemed to think were your own personal playground."

Ward hadn't been tossed out of the building, but it had been close. When he'd asked about his car, the security guard had flipped him a quarter and told him to call a cab. He'd walked back to his apartment to find that not only had they taken all his nice things, but his underwear as well. What the hell had his brother done with his underwear? It had taken him calling in a great many favors, as well as getting into the stash he'd had hidden in another place, to get back to where he thought he should have been, but it had never been the way things were. And now he was flying back to see him.

Ward was going to play nice. For a time, anyway, then he was going to stick it to his brother good. No one fucked with Ward Galloway and got away with it. Especially when it came to his lifestyle and his image. Image was everything.

The plane landed an hour later.

Ward had been staying with a friend of a friend when he'd gotten the call from Morton. It couldn't have come at a better time, either, because he was pretty sure he'd worn out his welcome. His so-called friends were telling him to get a job and to start helping out with bills and such. Not to mention it would be nice if he paid back what he had borrowed from them. This was going to be his ninth move in the past year, and it seemed to him that his pickings were getting slimmer and slimmer each time. But he had his list, and it wasn't to pay any of them back. It was to tell them what he'd taken from them without their knowledge.

Pulling it out now, he looked it over. It was a list of what he felt were crimes against him. He'd started out with a list of people he was going to pay back for all the help they'd given him, but it wasn't long when even those people had ended up on his other list. The list that kept running totals of women who wouldn't let him fuck them. Also, he had a list of men who had snubbed him at parties he'd crashed, as well as when he'd ask to borrow money. When one of them had asked him when he was going to pay them back, he'd only stared at the man. Did they really expect Ward Galloway to pay people back? This was just not done.

Standing in the terminal, Ward looked around for someone who would pick him up. There were all sorts of signs being held up with names printed on them, but none for him. Ward moved to the front of the airport and out into the driving rain. He shivered in his suit, wondering where the hell he was supposed to go now.

He had cab money, but he wasn't going to spend it unless he had to. And that possibility was looking stronger and stronger with each passing minute. Going back inside, he went to the terminal and had Morton paged. It was a big airport and maybe the old fucker got lost in there. After forty minutes of waiting and two pages for him later, he knew that he'd been forgotten. Time to take a cab.

But to where? Ward was going to stay with Morton until his brother invited him to stay with him, or at the very least gave him enough money to get a house or something. He didn't want a large house, just ten or so bedrooms so he could party when he wanted. And he needed enough to pay for the help it would require to keep it up. And he wanted pretty, fuckable bitches too. Ward didn't want to have to clean up after himself. Having fuckable bitches cleaning up after you was what having money was all about.

He was slipping in the dirty cab when he pulled out his phone again and called Morton's house. This time no one answered and he decided that he'd simply go there and wait. And if Morton didn't show up, he'd make due until something better came along. Besides, tomorrow he was going to see his brother. Then things would be just the way they should be for him. Ward Galloway was going to be something. And his long-lost fucking bastard of a brother was going to make it happen for him. Even if he didn't know it just yet.

~~~

Thad walked around the site twice. There was something so appealing to him to start a fresh project. And this one was going to be huge. The amount of people that would need to be hired for this portion of the business was going to help the area out and make it so he could keep his hands in his business. He looked up when Blair walked toward him.

"The land is being held by the bank, pending the judgment against the owner. He bilked nearly ten million from the bank on this deal, so you can imagine they're just a little skittish about letting it go without proof that this time the deal is going to be solid." Thad could understand that and waited for him to continue. "Along with the five hundred acres, there are the three partial buildings that I would simply tear down, as well as an additional seventy-five acres that has a house on it. The house is in good repair, if only needing a few updates. It's been sitting empty for nearly two years, with the exception of the staff that has been living there because they've had nowhere else to go. The bank decided that them staying there was better than leaving it empty."

"And they own the house too?" Blair nodded. "Can I get it as a package deal? And if so, how far are we going to be from the main house you live in?"

The property was perfect for what he wanted it for even though it was a little bigger than he'd wanted. But if things went well in a few years, he could bring the plant in Texas up here and have it all under one roof. When Blair didn't answer him, he looked at him.

While Blair hadn't been rude, he'd not been all that friendly either. Thad could understand that as well. He'd hurt them, all of them, and he was going to have to work very hard to get at least some of that friendship back. When there was still nothing from him, Thad spoke.

"I'm going to make this work with Diamond and the rest of you. I know that you have no reason to believe me, but—"

"I don't." Well, that was blunt, Thad thought, but didn't say anything as Blair continued. "You hurt her again and they'll never find the body. And I don't mean because I'll toss you in a deep hole. I mean there won't be anything of you left to find. Not even a bone fragment. I will tear you to little pieces, then let the others have at you."

Thad shivered at his words, knowing that he wasn't kidding at all. "I know what I've done and what I've said. You've no idea how much...you coming out here with me today means a great deal to me after the way I treated you. I will make this work. I'm doing my best to convince Diamond of it as well, but, like you, she's not going to forgive me right now." Thad looked out over the buildings and the land. "I had a long talk with Jane last night after Diamond went to sleep. She was telling me that I was lucky you hadn't killed me the last time I was here."

"I knew she was a smart woman." Blair laughed a little. "I don't think Diamond is going to be as easy to convince as I might be. You and she are going to have some rounds, and I hope I'm there to see it."

They'd had a round last night. She'd wanted him to sleep elsewhere, and he'd been serious about sleeping with her. But when she shifted into her wolf, he'd left the room quietly. She was fucking scary as that big canine.

"She can hold her own." Blair laughed at him again. "Your dad is very helpful. I asked him a few things yesterday that I didn't understand in the book, and he said I should bring them up to you. Can I ask you some of them now?"

"Sure, but you need to know that I don't know a great deal about being a pack alpha. I sort of fell into the job. I challenged the other leader because at the time I thought I'd be better than he was, but he died and I had to learn or fail. I don't like to fail."

Thad nodded. He didn't either, so he could empathize with the man.

"Did you know that you can't have your pack house and your home in the same residence?" Blair looked at him with a frown. "It says that you and your mate have to live separate from the pack house. I don't think many do it, but that's one of the rules."

"Did it say why?" Thad had thought that Blair would tell him he was lying or, worse, that he would tell him he knew but didn't care. He wanted to know that the man that he'd call alpha someday had integrity.

"It actually gives several reasons, but the main one is because you can't leave yourself in an unprotected environment in the event that one of your pack turns rogue. Apparently, there have been several cases, and in recent years, where one of the pack goes a little over the deep end and walked through the house killing everyone until he got to the alpha and his family. It wasn't pretty." Thad shivered again when he thought of the accounting of the massacre. "There is also something about having your family away from the everyday things of being an alpha so that they can have a life with you or, in this case, with you and Sapphire, that doesn't revolve around pack all the time."

"Why?" Thad and he were walking back to Blair's truck when he asked him. Thad started to ask him what he meant when he continued. "Why are you telling me this? You could have easily gotten me into trouble with the Board. Are you sucking up? I can tell you now it won't work. I've fired people for that."

"No, I've no reason to suck up. I'm going to make my own way here with or without your permission or help. But I'm a rules kind of guy and when I see them being broken by no other fault than because someone didn't know, I bring it up. What you do or don't do with the information is entirely up to you." Thad moved to the other side of the truck, somewhat hurt by Blair's question.

When he was seated inside the monster thing, he buckled in and waited for Blair to get going.

"I'm not good at this male bonding thing. I say what I want, not thinking about how my words will affect others. Sapphire has made it her life's work to point this out to me whenever she can. This, I might add, is hourly. What I should have said was thank you and I'll make it better. And for the record, I want this thing to work too. I've missed your friendship and your sense of humor. You're not all bad for a human."

Thad was shocked. Not pissed, but completely and utterly shocked. Blair had just called him a human like it was something he found under his shoe. Then he winked. Thad looked out the window and tried to wrap his mind around what just happened. He thought that he'd just been forgiven. When he looked at Blair again, he realized something else. He was a human and Blair was not.

Before he could comment, though he wasn't sure what he might have said, Thad's phone went off. When he heard the tone, his first thoughts were what Morton had done now to piss Jane off, when he remembered that Morton was no longer a problem. He was smiling when he answered.

"I've found the area for the plastics plant. The bank has a house as well that might go along with it." Thad started to tell her the rest when she interrupted him.

"Ward is here." His entire body went on red alert. "Not in the building but in the area. He called here about ten minutes ago looking for you and asking if he was able to get back in the building as yet. I started to tell him hell no, but decided I'd ask you about it first. You didn't take him back did you?"

"No. No, I didn't." He glanced at Blair and realized that he could hear the conversation and put it on speakerphone. "I'm with Blair in the truck. Tell me what you told Ward."

"Hello, Blair. I told him that I'd have to contact you to see what you'd set up. I was reasonably sure that the only thing you would have set up with the little pisser was him staying the fuck away but...well hell, I needed to hear it from your own lips." Thad was trying to think what Ward wanted when Blair spoke to Jane.

"Does he know where Thad is now?" Jane said not as far as she knew. "Good. I'm not sure what's going on with this person, but I'm assuming he's not anyone we want to visit here."

"Ward Galloway is my brother. And if there were a more selfish prick in this world, I'm not sure I'd want to meet him. He took over six million in cash and other things when it was all said and done, and I was only able to get about a quarter of that back." Thad didn't want to think about this right now. "If he comes here, trouble will follow. For whatever reason, he's got it in his head that because I have money he can pretty much spend as much as he wants and I not say a word. I've worked very hard for every penny I've got and he seemed to think that because he was a Galloway, he should have all I had too."

"What would you like me to do? Take care of him and put him beside our good friend Morton? I can do that." Thad started to scream at her no when she laughed. "I'm kidding, boss. Don't get your panties in an uproar. I've put a man on him to find out where he's staying, and I've also started a check on what he's been doing for the past ten years. From the way he was dressed, I don't think things are as good as he wants them to be. And I'm reasonably sure that he had big plans for you as well."

"No doubt." Thad leaned his head back against the seat and tried to think what to do. "Just keep me informed, and when he comes back, just let him know that you're still trying to find me. That I'm on some sort of...I don't know, vacation."

Jane laughed hard. "*You* on a vacation? He'll never believe that any more than anyone else that works for you would. You are not a vacation sort of person. Why don't I tell him you're on a business trip? It's the truth and he'll have to sit still until we figure out what to do about him."

After he ended the call, he looked at Blair. "I'm going to have to tell you all what he's like so that in the event he does make the connection to here you'll know what to do about him."

Blair nodded before saying anything. "I'm thinking you should have your house upgraded soon. I have a few pack members that can do the job for you as soon as the bank gives you the go ahead. Not that I don't think you and Diamond can take him on, but I don't want to take the chances with my family."

Family. Thad had one now. Oh, he had a brother, but he was more of a problem than he was anything else. He told Blair he would do what it took.

"Do you think we can swing by the bank? And I need to make another stop too. I want to get Diamond a ring, and no offense to your dad, I'd rather you went with me than him." They were still laughing when they entered the bank ten minutes later.

Chapter 9

"I just don't understand why you want to speak to the head of the hospital." Diamond didn't repeat herself again to her old boss. "I can answer just about any questions you might have about working for me."

"I'd be working for the hospital, not you." Jan was walking just ahead of her or she might have missed her slight hobble in her step. "I said I'd come back, but speaking to him is important. And as I said before, I'll do so alone or not at all."

When Jan turned to her, Diamond could see the anger blazing in her eyes. There was no way she was going to work for someone like her without knowing where she stood. The woman was a tyrant, and Diamond had it on good authority from a few other nurses, they'd had enough of her as well. Time to take a stand or work at doing something else.

The brisk knock at the door had her going in behind the doctor. Mr. Cable Jansen stood up just as she closed the door behind her. Diamond didn't move from her position at the door, thinking if this didn't go her way, she was out of there.

"I understand you've gotten all your problems at home taken care of now. I'm so glad to hear that." Diamond looked at Jan when Cable continued. "Sometimes all it takes is a few days off to settle all the turmoil that can seem so overwhelming."

"I told Mr. Jansen that you were taking a leave. Like you told me you were." Jan had added just enough stress in her voice to try to get Diamond to back her up. Well, she wasn't playing her games any longer.

"There was nothing wrong at home, Mr. Jansen, I quit. Doctor Talley here was the issue." Both he and Jan looked shocked. "I'd like to come back to work here, but there are conditions I'd very much like to discuss with you in private if possible."

"I think I should hear this." Jan crossed her arms over her chest and glared at her. "If you're going to lie about me, then I should be privy to the—"

"You mean lie like you did about me leaving here? No thanks. As I said downstairs as well as on the elevator ride up here, I would like to speak to Mr. Jansen alone. That means without you present." They both turned to look at Mr. Jansen, who seemed confused as well as a little upset. "If you'd rather not, sir, I can understand. I can work elsewhere if you have an issue with—"

"Oh no, it's not that at all. It's just that…perhaps you should go, Doctor Talley. If I need you, I know where to find you." Mr. Jansen turned his back to them both, seemingly dismissing the doctor. Diamond waited for her to say something else to her, but she only turned on her heel and left the room. The door sounded hard as she slammed it behind her.

"I think we've made an enemy in her." Mr. Jansen smiled. "Have a seat, Diamond…I may call you Diamond, correct?"

"Yes." Diamond sat in the chair across from his desk and was a little disconcerted when he sat in the one next to her. "She's a good doctor, but a bitch to the nurses."

When he laughed, she flushed. She'd never been good at beating around the bush and apologized to him immediately. He waved her off.

"You are refreshing in your honesty. Tell me why you call her that. And for the record, I think you might be right. I've had a few complaints from the other nurses since you've quit." He smiled gently at her. "Yes, I'm aware of you quitting. I'm glad you decided to give us another try before moving to New York."

She didn't even ask him how he knew. Diamond had filled out the application and they would have contacted him for her references. Reaching into her pocket, she pulled out the list of her "demands."

"I think you're going to lose a great bunch of nurses if you keep her on staff in the emergency room. We know our job for the most part." She looked down at her notes, then up at him. "No, that's a lie. You'll lose some mediocre nurses if she stays down there. For the most part, you have one or two nurses on all the shifts combined that do a half-assed job, and the rest are worthless."

"While I appreciate you being honest with me, I think you have a great deal more stored up in your mind. Tell me why this is true." She didn't really think that he wanted her to be honest, but thought that she'd do it anyway. What the hell did she have to lose by telling him that Jan Talley was a power junkie, and that if things didn't go her way all the time, others would suffer?

For over two hours she told him of things she'd witnessed. "Jan also has a tendency to belittle others, nurses, in front of other staff and patients. It's sort of become legend with her that if she doesn't dress you down in front of someone daily, you're no longer worth her time and will be fired within the week. I myself have seen it happen to good nurses."

"You think this is why we only have the lower end of the scale working for us?" She nodded. "What would you do? If you were in charge of the nurses, what would you do to make it so we got a better quality of nurses and keep them? I mean long term."

"I'm sure you know that better pay would be great, but aside from that, you need to have better working conditions. Such as places for us to have a break...and I mean one away from the doctors, a place they can't come into. There has to be somewhere we can vent, even if it is about them." She looked around his office before she said what she really wanted. "I would like to be put in charge of the nursing staff. All the shifts too."

He smiled at her before getting up and sitting behind his desk. "I believe that someone needs to be in that position that can take charge and make them want to come to work. Also, this person will need to be able to stand up to the doctors and keep them from becoming a tyrant, making and attracting better nurses who know that someone is in their corner. I didn't think you were that sort of person."

She nodded and stood up. "Then I thank you for your time. I do wish you the best of luck in the future. I honestly do."

"Diamond?" She turned back to look at him before she touched the door handle. "I don't *think* you're that sort of person, I *know* you are. You're the best this hospital has ever had, and I believe your sister is going to make a great doctor as well. An unstoppable team if you want to know the truth of it." He grinned at her. "Do you not want the job?"

~~~

Ward waited in the small conference room for nearly twenty minutes before he decided that he'd had enough. This was just stupid, and if they thought they could treat him this way, he'd have to show them that he wasn't a pushover any longer. His brother owned the fucking company for Christ's sake. They had another think coming if they thought they could just shove him in a corner and forget about him. He moved to the door just as it opened. The fucking bitch Jane was there. He hated her with a passion.

"You're very lucky I was able to track your brother down." She pointed to the chair he'd just vacated as she continued. "I did tell you the other day when you were here that he was out of the country, correct?"

"You said he was on a business trip. Why the hell he doesn't have somebody else to that kind of shit for him is beyond me. He should have been here when I got here." Ward flopped in the chair and glared at her. "You told him I was here and he's on his way back, I assume?"

"You assume wrong. He's on a business trip, as I've said to you several times now. And you know as well as I do, when he's onto something he takes care of it. Unlike some people I know." He decided to ignore her dig at him.

"Then when is he coming back here? I need to see him…there are things that he doesn't know about me that I…." He got up to pace, not caring for the way she kept smiling at him. "I'm a changed man. I've gotten my life together and put things in perspective."

"Sure you have. And where is it you're staying while in town? I can smell Morton all over you, and since I know you've not met up with him, I can only assume you're staying in his house." Ward stared at her, wondering how the hell she'd figured that out. "Then there's the smell of coke on you. Why would a man who professes to have his life together come to a meeting as high as a kite?"

"You called me after I'd taken the hit. I can't be held responsible if you don't give me enough notice on things like this." He started pacing again and tried his best to pull his temper back in. She wasn't helping with her soft little laughs at him and the way she kept at him over and over.

"Sit down." There was a tone there that Ward didn't care for, but he knew that if he didn't sit she'd somehow hurt him. While he didn't mind the occasional pain, there was just something very scary about her right now.

"I demand that you tell me where Thad is. I will go to him and see about getting this shit cleared up so I can start getting a paycheck." When Jane threw back her head and laughed at him, Ward had the most terrifying thought pop in his head. She had fangs.

"You're going to stop coming here unless I call you to come in. And when I do, you'll be respectful of the people who work here. Understand me?" He nodded, unable not to. "And when I call you in, you're going to be sober, as well as clean of drugs. If you have them in your system, you tell me so and I'll arrange to have the meeting at a later time."

"I need money." She shook her head at him. "There was some at Morton's house, but not enough for me to live on until Thad comes back."

"I'll take care of the bills for the house for now, but nothing more. You want money for drugs, you'll have to earn it. I'm not going to—"

Ward forgot about his fear for a few seconds and stood up to knock her on her ass. When she snarled at him, showing him that she really did have those sharp fangs, he sat back down and froze in his chair. Fear made him clench his ass as well as his fists, and he was terrified that he was going to wet himself. He didn't even look up at her when she stood up and paced where he'd been before.

"The only thing saving your ass right now from joining Morton is the fact that Thad asked me not to harm you. Well, not really, but he didn't give me the okay to kill you when I asked." Ward glanced up at her and then dropped his head when he saw that now not only did she have fangs, but her eyes were red. Not bloodshot like his were most of the time, but a true red. Sweat ran down his spine, and he felt a chill in the air. When she snapped his head back by jerking his hair, Ward whimpered like a child. He knew the sound; he'd made plenty of children do it in his lifetime.

"Do you know how hungry you make me with your pounding heart and fear spiking your blood?" She licked along his pounding pulse and moaned. Ward felt his bladder let go, and he didn't even care at this point.

"Are you going to kill me?" His voice sounded whiny and childlike. He hated it, but he was glad for the moment that she didn't tear his throat out. But when she lowered her head and he felt a pinch at his throat, Ward knew he was a dead man. Jane lifted her head and licked her lips before she took a step back from him.

"Delicious." She sat down in a chair as far from him as she could and still be in the same room before she continued. "I've drank from you. Not nearly as much as I'd like, mind you, but enough to know your every move, your every thought."

Ward nodded and tried to think what the fuck she was talking about. Thad, he thought, he was doing this to him. Making him fearful and terrified so he'd do what he wanted. When Jane spoke, he was no longer really listening. He was thinking of ways to get back at them both, Jane and his brother, for putting him through this. When he realized he was alone, he got up and looked down at himself. There was a dark stain on him, but he'd also ruined the chair, and the carpet would need to be cleaned as well. Deciding that he might as well mark the rest of the room, he was just unbuckling his belt when the door opened. A security guard was standing there with his gun pointed at him.

"You think to shoot me?" The man shrugged. "I wouldn't advise that course of action if I were you. I know people. My brother owns this place, and he'll be pissed if you harm me."

"You think I give a good shit if your brother is a little upset about me messing up his office? Hell, I'd probably get a raise.

You get yourself on out of here and I'll make sure you get out of the building all nice and safely." The man made it sound like his safety wasn't all that much of a concern of his and proved it when he shoved Ward against the wall and then onto the elevator floor when it finally opened.

"I'm going to report you." The man shrugged again. "You'll see that you get into major trouble with Thad when he comes here for me." Suddenly, Ward found himself against the elevator wall about three feet off the ground. He jerked and pulled on the hand at his throat, but the man was simply too strong.

As he walked him through the lobby like this, Ward was beginning to see stars. He was going to pass out long before he was let go, he just knew it. When he was free, the ground came up and slammed him hard, and he lay on the sidewalk looking up at the sky while he tried to wrap his mind around what the fuck had just happened.

As Ward made his way to the car he'd taken from Morton's garage, he started to replay the things that had happened in his mind. First and foremost was Jane. Did she really have fangs or did she have those fake ones he'd had as a kid at Halloween? Likely. She was just a plain Jane. He laughed at his own joke as he stopped at a light. And her biting him. Not fucking true. How the hell did he even think that? She's pinched him, just as he'd thought she'd done, that's all.

And the security guard? Nobody could lift him that far off the ground. It was his mind, which had been full of coke, playing tricks on him. Smiling as he continued to go along the road back to his home, he realized that his brother was more than likely in the fucking place too. His brother was in his office right now laughing it up with Jane on how she'd made him so afraid...no, not afraid, but nervous. She'd made him so nervous that he'd left without looking for Thad. Ward looked down at his pants and snorted. Somebody was going to pay for pouring some shit on him.

Ward had it all straight in his head now. Thad was in big trouble if he thought that he was going to get away with treating him this way. He was Ward Galloway, and no one, not even his own blood, was going to do this and get away with it.

There was a note stuck to the door when he got back. Morton either had to pay up on the electric bill or he was in danger of being cut off. He did remember Janey girl saying something about paying the bills. He wadded it up and tossed it on the floor. Going into the house, he headed straight for the kitchen and opened the refrigerator.

"Nothing." Ward moved what appeared to be several hundred Chinese containers out of the way to unearth a bottle of cheap wine and a single can of ale. "You're killing me here, Mortorie old man. When you have a guest coming, put in the good stuff."

Taking out all the containers and setting them on the counter, he started sniffing them until he nearly made himself ill from it. These things were all bad, and he didn't have anything to eat. Not even bothering with a glass, Ward started to go through the cabinets to find at least something to eat as he finished off the liquor. There were a few things he could cook and eat, but he'd never been one for doing for himself. He'd have to either hire a chick to cook for him, which right now was not a financial option, or he could simply find a job. Earning money to order in sounded good to a point, but then he'd have to go and do work, not anything he wanted to do.

Going to the living room, he sat in front of the television and started surfing the channels. When he found a game on, he stopped to watch it. But before he could figure it out, like what the announcer was saying, his phone went off.

His greeting was cut short by an automated woman. She informed him in her nasal monotone voice that if payment were not made to pay the bill in full, there was a good possibility of him having his service disconnected. Ward shouted in the phone before she finished.

"Don't you know who I am," he asked his phone. "I'm Ward Galloway, brother to Thad Galloway. I'm the richest man in the world."

When he put the phone back to his ear, she was still droning on about bills and obligations. He ended the call and tossed the phone on the dirty table in front of him. Ward couldn't even remember the last time he'd paid his bill, or any bills for that matter. As a matter of fact, he didn't even know whose account his phone was on.

Picking it up again, he listened to the messages he had and found one that told him to call a three digit number. Dialing it, he was asked to wait. An hour later, nearly asleep in the chair, someone finally came on. And no matter how pissed he got with her, the woman would not give up the name on the account.

"But who do I have to call to get them to pay this?" She huffed at him. He'd asked her the same question five times already. "Someone had to be paying it before now."

"They dropped you from their plan. Eleven months ago, as a matter of fact, and unfortunately for us, we've only just caught it." Before he could ask her how the hell that was his fault, she started talking again. "We're going to need for you to pay the past due balance of three thousand four hundred eighty-three dollars and one cent. Once that is paid in full, we'll turn your service back on. Would you like to pay that with a credit card or a virtual check from your bank?"

"How about I pay that with a go fuck yourself!" Ward said and hung up. What the fuck? Where the hell was he supposed to get that much money? Thad's list of shit that Ward was going to demand he fix was mounting up. And that one cent bothered him more than the entire balance for some reason.

"One cent. Like that fucking makes a big difference." He went to the kitchen to start a list. There was no time like the present to get started on things for his big brother to take care of. "Fucking one cent."

Chapter 10

Thad wasn't sure what was going on, but the bank manager was taking a great deal longer than he thought necessary to call his bank back home and get back to him. He glanced over at Blair, who seemed to be talking to someone but without a phone. He realized that he was more than likely talking to Sapphire, and thought about Diamond.

The connection between them was stronger than it had been before. He'd been able to talk to her, of course, but now he could almost see her standing in front of him. When he reached for her in his mind, he felt her arousal. His entire body hardened at the thought of her. She must have felt it as well.

What do you think you're doing? I'm in the middle of the grocery store. Behave yourself. He smiled at her tone. *What are you doing? I thought you were going to look at that site for the new building?*

I am or I was. Actually, right now I'm sitting in the bank waiting for the manager to get back here and tell me that I own it. There was a house attached to it as well. What do you think about owning a house about five minutes from your family?

She didn't answer him right away, but he wasn't worried. She was in the store, perhaps she was speaking to someone. Thad watched the manager come toward him and could see the look of relief on his face. No doubt having this property off their books was going to help a great many people.

I have a job now. I'm going to be starting it in three weeks. They have to make up a contract for me. I'm head nurse for the entire staffing at the hospital. I'll be working through the weekday and have my weekends off. Thad waited knowing that she was working up to something. *I'll be able to help you make payments on something but only if it's not too big. I have some student loans I'm still paying off, and I will need a more reliable car.* Thad asked her to wait a moment as the banker was speaking to him.

"Mr. Galloway, I'm sorry I took so long, but I only realized at the moment your lender started talking who you were. I'm terribly sorry to have made you wait." Thad shook his head at him. "The land you asked to purchase is yours if you wish. The house, as a part of the settlement, is also available. Though it has been sitting mostly empty all this time, we have maintained it to the minimum standards."

Thad had a feeling that minimum standards would have an entirely different meaning between the two of them. "I'd very much like to see it before I make an offer on the house. My...future wife will also want to make sure it's what we want."

Thad tried hard not to look at Blair as he laughed. He had a feeling that as soon as Diamond found out how he'd referred to her she wouldn't think it was so funny.

"Of course, of course. I can have someone go over with you as soon as you'd like. There are just a few things I'd like to point out about the property and house. Minor things that you should be made aware of. They aren't things that will—"

"Just tell me." The bank manager nodded, making the fat under his several chins wobble. When he flushed brightly, Thad was ready to tell him that the entire deal was off. Nothing that took this long could be good.

"What do you know of the house, sir?" Thad told him nothing. "Well, sir, it's very large. I don't mean just the land around it but the house itself is...the house is just less than sixty thousand square feet."

Thad looked at Blair, who sat up with him. This wasn't a house he was buying, it was a fucking mansion. He took the file that the manager handed him. There were pictures of the grounds and some of the drive up to the house. When he got to the one of the home itself, he looked at the manager again.

"I'm sorry, what was your name again? I think this...this is a great deal more than I had first thought." The manager nodded as if he understood and told him his name. "Well, Mr. Robert Beck, I'd very much like to see the house now if possible."

"You still wish to entertain the thoughts of buying it?" The incredulity of the man's voice was nearly comical. "I had thought...well we could never seem to know why the previous owners would want to...."

"I wish to see the house. When can it be arranged?" Thad stood up and reached for Diamond. *Diamond, love, I was wondering if you were busy at the moment. I would like to go and see a house and would very much like your input.*

Why? Thad had to laugh. This woman was never going to be just a simple yes woman, at least not outside the bedroom. *You're perfectly capable of looking at your own house all by yourself.*

Because I would like for you to see it with me. Work with me, Diamond, we're a couple and I'd very much like it if the house we buy is something that we both agree on. He reached for the keys that Blair handed him. *I'm going to send a car for you. Would that be all right?*

I have a car. I can meet you there. Just tell me...you never said anything about me having a job. I won't quit just because you think you have all the money in the world. Blair told him he had to go by the house, and he'd let him and Diamond look at it first but wanted to see it even if they didn't buy the sucker.

I don't have all the money in the world, but I am very wealthy. Both of us are. He heard her sputter and cut her off gently. *I don't care if you work. In fact, I love that you want to continue doing what you love. I'm also happy that you'll have weekends off with me. We're going to need more time to get to know each other. But it isn't necessary that you work, just so you know that.*

It's necessary for me. He could understand that as well and told her so. *I know this is really crass of me but just how much are you talking about? Money, I mean. I know Blair has a lot. He is reported to be worth several million dollars.*

We have a great deal more. She didn't speak, nor did he feel a connection to her. And since Blair had left him, he had no way of asking what was going on. When Diamond finally spoke, he was in his car ready to go to her.

A great deal more, meaning you have a great deal more money or you have a great deal more of everything? I'm not sure what the differences are but...Christ, a great deal more, really?

Yes. We're worth just over eighty billion dollars in just personal assets. The company is separate from the personal money because I incorporated several years ago. The business, Galloway Industries, has several hundred smaller companies under it which all answer to me...well, now us. The business part of our money is just—

Don't tell me. Just knowing that you're worth eighty billion...how many zeros is that anyway? He started to tell her that there were nine if you didn't count the one in eighty, but she started talking again. *I'm going to meet you there, but I need an address, and if this house is really big, I may have to have you give me mouth to mouth.*

Thad felt his cock leap in his pants. *Giving you anything you want that involves my mouth and your body would be my upmost pleasure.*

Glad now that he'd gotten someone to drive him around the unfamiliar city, he leaned back in the seat after telling her the address. *Do you have any idea what I'd like to be doing to you right now? And if this house becomes ours in the next few days, I'm going to have us a little play room put in.*

I don't know how to play like you do. I've barely had sex, much less had someone do the things that players do to each other. He felt her embarrassment as well as her arousal again. *I did some research today before I went to the interview with the hospital.*

And what did you find? Do you think it would be something you'd enjoy? She didn't say anything back and he was slightly nervous. There are many levels of sexual pleasure we can bring to each other. *We can start very slow and make our way up until you get comfortable.*

Are you going to really use a paddle on me? Thad stroked his cock when she asked. Christ, he could almost come right now. *I've seen where the master can leave painful bruises on his sub. I don't think I'd ever want to go as far as some of those people do.*

I like to make you obey, have you not come for sometimes days, but I'd never leave you marked like that. I will hurt you if you'll let me. Tie you to the cross I plan to buy for us, but not enough where it would mar your lovely skin. I love the way your body looks now. He moved his hand up and down over his cock wanting to free himself and think of her and their newest room. *I would love to use a feather on your pussy. You'd be surprised at how much pleasure I can bring you with something as simple as that.*

Will you let me tie you down? I'd like to explore you knowing that you can't touch me. Thad was going to have to do something soon or he wasn't going to be able to walk when he finally had to stand. *Thad, I'm at the house. I don't...are we actually going to look at this monster? We could live here for months and never see each other. Christ, it's bigger than the hospital.*

His car came to a smooth stop and he got out before the driver could help him. Thad saw her standing next to a very late model two door that looked like it might have been red at one time but was now a sort of puke brown. Walking up behind her, he noticed that she had on a short skirt and a blouse that showed more curves than he wanted others to see. He wrapped his hand around her waist and pulled her to him, and she looked up at him.

"I'm not cleaning this place. It will take me a week just to get from one end of the house to the other with a map." Kissing her seemed the best way to end her panic, and he took her into his arms.

Thad was thinking how difficult it would be to take her against her little car when he heard someone pull up behind them. When Diamond growled low, he nearly told her to forget the house and find a dark area where he could take her when they turned to look at Mr. Beck.

"Big isn't it?" Neither of them said anything to the man, and he nodded. "Well, let's go inside shall we?"

~~~

The house was much bigger on the inside than it looked on the out. And she was absolutely in love with it. There were rooms as big as her dorm room in college and some as big as her dorm house. Diamond wandered into the main hall and looked up at the spiral staircase. She was trying to figure out if she wanted to venture that far when Thad came up behind her.

"Going up?" She didn't answer him. "We can simply tell him we want it sight unseen if you want."

"Did you see the size of that dining room? We could entertain a small country in there." He nodded at her shoulder, and when his arms wrapped around her waist, she stood still. "I like the house, but I don't know if we need this much."

"I'm just glad to hear you say we don't need it. And as much as I hate to bring this up, with money comes the added responsibility of entertaining clients. I've not had to do much of it in the past simply because I didn't want to, but with you I'd really like to show you off. And you love the house." She turned in his arms and looked up at him. "What?"

"You want to show me off? Not as a wolf, right?" He smiled at her and she shook her head. "I'm going to be a real embarrassment to you if someone expects me to be something spectacular. I'm just Diamond Erickson, registered nurse."

"Head nurse. And so you know, to me you're pretty close to spectacular." He kissed her on the nose and took her hand. "Come on, Robert is getting antsy. Let's have a look at the other floors before he begs us to have a look at the sub levels again."

She'd nearly fallen over when she'd gone down to what she'd thought of as a basement. It was anything but a basement. It was a huge ballroom complete with its own kitchen and semi-truck entrance for bringing in food. She had walked into the large room complete with tables and chairs that had been left behind and were part of the house, as was all the furniture, and stared open mouthed. Robert had told them that they could seat three hundred guests inside and an additional one hundred when the side doors to the patio were opened.

In addition to the ballroom there was a conference room that could seat as many as fifty and as few as ten that had a large smart board, stereo system, as well as large picture windows that ran along one entire wall that had a view of the woods and lake behind the house. There was even an entrance to the sub levels that could make it so that no one had to enter through the main house to get inside.

The main level of the house was no less impressive. The main entryway was domed with oak beams and arched doorways. The chandelier was as big as her car and probably weighed more. When it had been turned on by Robert, it sparkled around the large room so brilliantly that she was reminded of a Christmas tree. Three doorways led out into the three different parts of the main house.

The right led to a large office library. The shelves were stocked full of old and new books the banker had told him were just too valuable to let go at auction. But if they decided to buy the house, they, too, would be part of the entire house. As was every room in the house, this one was fully furnished. The desk alone could serve as a massive bed if they could find a mattress large enough.

The left side of the hall opened into a large sitting area. Robert had called it parlor, but she thought of it as a reception area. There were small sitting areas spread out over the large room, which boosted three fire places and four of the biggest doors she'd ever seen. They spilled out onto the deck that surrounded the entire side of the house.

The middle door opened into an expansive staircase. It was as wide as twenty feet and branched off into three areas when you got to the first landing. They hadn't gone up there yet, but she'd been told what she'd find. The branches led to the separate wings of the house that spread out from the house, making a half circle around the deck and pool that could be accessed by any of the lower rooms, including the kitchen.

"Want to go up?" Did she? Not really. She'd already fallen in love with the house, and the upstairs was just going to be more of the same. Diamond knew that he could well afford the house, but what happened when he decided to move back to Texas? She didn't think she'd be able to afford the electric bill, much less the house payment. She followed him up the stairs.

There were six bedrooms to the left, all of them with a private bath as well as closet spaces large enough to hold the entire inventory of a store. She walked along the middle bedroom and ran her fingers over the beautiful chest of drawers that was between two large windows across from the bed. Diamond looked at Thad when he cleared his throat.

"What do you really think of the house?" Diamond looked around this room. A little girl's room, she'd bet. Even without the personal things, there were enough small touches to show that a girl had used this one.

"What would we do with it? I mean, it's lovely...no, it's beautiful, and I love it, but it's really large. Bigger than I think we'd need for entertaining." Thad didn't move from his position at the door, so she sat on the bed to continue. "We're a couple who are together because of fate. Not because we love each other, not even because we like one another. We're just...here."

"Do you want to fall in love with me?" His voice was soft and soothing over her. When she didn't answer, she watched him walk toward her in a smooth, almost wolf-like move. Her body temperature skyrocketed, and he paused.

"Can you feel that?" He nodded. "It's my wolf. She's not as shy as I'd be if I knew how to be seductive."

"You think you're not seductive? Christ, baby, I only have to think of you and I'm hard." He rubbed his hand down his cock. "I've been hard since I saw you when we pulled up, even before that actually. And I was trying to think of a way to get you bent over anything that could hold up to the pounding I wanted to give you when Robert showed up."

He was nearly to her when she felt her wolf skim along her skin. She wanted to mark her mate too, but Diamond wasn't sure Thad would want that. Fingers danced softly along her skin at her throat, and she moaned when he kissed her.

"I want you right now." Nodding, she let him lay her back on the bed. "I sent Robert outside so that we could explore the house on our own. Do you think you can wait long enough for us to go to where the master suite is? I have plans for your delectable body."

When his body covered hers for a few seconds, she felt every nerve ending come to life. As he lifted from her, she reached for him to pull him back when she suddenly found herself on her feet.

"It's at the end of the hall and to your right. Go now before I tear your clothes from you and you're left standing here naked." She took off toward the door. "Be naked when I get there too."

Her heart was pounding by the time she found the room. Diamond nearly fell over when she saw how big the bed was and stopped to stare. But then she heard Thad coming down the hall and tore her clothing off and tossed them everywhere to get to where he'd told her. She was just lying on the bare mattress when he stepped in the room.

"I wish I had time to make you needy, but I've wanted to be deep inside of you for days." She lay back when he stood over her. "Spread your legs for me."

She did what he asked without hesitation. He dropped before her and opened her wider with his finger, and she felt her juices flow. When he hummed, she knew that he could see her fully. Thad licked her from gate to clit. She cried out, the feel of his tongue so intimately against her making her want more.

"Do you want me to fuck you or eat you?" Christ, she was on fire for either. "I can't do both because I have a feeling that Robert will come looking for us if I do."

"Please, fuck me." He stood up and opened his pants. Reaching for him, he rocked into her hand as she pulled him to her mouth. The pearl of cum on the tip of his thick head had her sucking hard for more.

"Christ, you're going to make me come down your throat and I need to fuck you." He continued to rock into her mouth as she cupped his balls. "Diamond, I'm going to make you pay for this."

Diamond didn't care. She loved the feel of him in her mouth, and when he cupped the back of her head and held her to him, she moaned. The harder he rocked the more she wanted to have him come this way. When his fingers tightened painfully in her hair, she nearly let him go. His strangled cry was all the warning she got before she tasted him.

Dizziness swamped her as he filled her. She couldn't breathe well, but even that didn't bother her. As he pulled away from her, she growled low, but he rolled her over to her belly before she could beg him for more.

The growled "on your hands" had her scrambling to do as he bid. By the time she'd figured out what he'd wanted, Thad had pulled her up so that she leaned over the bed. His cock slammed into her so quickly that it took her breath away.

"I should make you suffer and not let you come. But I need to…Christ. The need to bite you is making me insane with need." She had the same need, to mark him as her own. When his mouth nipped at her shoulder, she arched up beneath him to give him just what he wanted. As soon as he started to move in and out of her with a speed that had her wolf snarl at him, she felt his mouth suck hard at her flesh.

"Lick it. Lick where you want to bite me." His tongue moving over her skin had her shiver. "When you bite, do it quick and hard, don't think about anything but tasting me, tasting my blood."

As soon as he tore into her, she buried her face in the mattress and screamed. Her climax tore through her like a tornado until she was rising for another and another. As her body continued to come, she felt the room dim and her body float when she felt him lick the wound he'd created closed. Her final thoughts were he'd been able to seal the wounds when he'd only been human.

Chapter 11

Ward was sitting across from his brother's building when he saw one of the men Morton had told him was a good guy come out. He moved across the street toward him, almost getting hit by a stupid driver in the process. What the fuck was wrong with these people? No one seemed to care at all who the hell he was. Ward moved up beside the man, not having a clue what his name was until he spied the badge on his shirt.

"Hello, Peter, remember me?" The man was nearly old enough to be his father, so when he smiled at him and nodded, Ward was relieved.

"You're that guy that Morton said was going to make us all rich." Frowning, he wondered about that for a second before Peter continued. "I haven't seen Morton for a while now. Is he with you?"

"No. I'm not sure...I've been staying at his house for a few days now. He said it would be okay until he came back. I guess he's...he went with my brother." Ward was glad that thought came to him just then, because Peter nodded. "I guess they've been on some business trip."

"Yeah. I guess after the accident he hung around for a few days but then he came back. Then not long after, we were told he was planning to open up the manufacturing plant in Ohio of all places." Peter shook his head as he opened his car door. "I thought for sure we were all gonna lose our jobs when he moved everything up there. Christ, I have a house and three kids in college down here. I can't just move to some small city like Zanesville, Ohio, at the drop of a hat. Then I guess his marketing team is there too, so I guess it wouldn't be too bad to have him out of the building more."

Ward wished he'd have brought a pen and paper now. The guy was a fountain of information and none of it he'd had to ask for. By the time Peter told him he had to get home, he had a wealth of information. Not only did Ward know where his brother was, but also the name of the marketing company he was using in Ohio, as well as how long he'd been gone. He wondered for a moment if he should have inquired after his brother's health about the accident, but Peter had never shut up long enough for him to do anything more than nod. Smiling, Ward made his way back to Morton's house.

There was little to nothing in the house to sell. And what there had been had gone up his nose this morning. He was searching around the bedroom again when he heard the doorbell ring. He never answered it unless he was sure who was coming, like the pizza person and such, but the last time she'd been there, something had pissed her off and she vowed never to return. All he'd done was ask the woman if she'd want to go down on him for her tip. What was the harm in asking if you didn't know?

There was a man in a suit at the door. Cautiously, Ward watched him for several seconds to see if he was the police or a bill collector when the guy said his name.

"Jane sent me. She said you were expecting me." He wasn't but opened the door anyway. "She said to tell you that this is the money for the phone as well as the house payment. Nothing more I'm supposed to tell you."

Ward snatched the envelopes in his hand and slammed the door shut in the man's face. Ward heard him laugh as he made his way to the kitchen but was already tearing open the first of five envelopes to see if the bitch had written checks or had given him cash. He did a jig around the kitchen when he found all of them held cash.

Laying it out on the dirty table, he counted it three times. There wasn't a lot, he thought. Probably just enough to get him to Ohio, but not back. He had no idea how much things cost because he never really bothered with the mundane things like paying for things when there was always some sucker that would do it for him. Ward glared at his phone that had been off now for three days. And there was no hope for him to get it back on until he saw his brother. Thad would have to take care of it for him just like he'd want him to.

Taking his dirty clothes to the airport seemed stupid to him, so he made his way to the first men's clothing store he could find. The suits were a little more than he wanted to spend on one, but he needed something that said I'm successful, not run-down and out of money. The sales person came up to him with a smile.

"They're nice, are they not? We can have it tailored for you in a few weeks if you'd like." Ward did want that, but waiting a few weeks was out of the question. He moved to another rack and was just pulling out a blue jacket when Bill (according to his name tag) was right there again.

"I'm really just looking." Bill nodded, but didn't move away. "Don't you have someone else you can bother? I said I'm just looking around."

"I can help you look if you'd like. I think you should look at the lavender shirt just on the rack near the back." Ward looked around the store, wondering if he could just hit the guy in the face and see if that got rid of him. "We're here all alone, and I could help you in any way you want."

A come on. The guy was coming on to him. Ward had an idea. He was strictly a heterosexual, but if he could flirt with Bill enough, maybe he'd give him a good deal on the suit. Nodding, Ward followed him back to the sale rack and watched as he sorted through the shirts.

"I'm looking for an entire suit. The one I have is a little on the worn side." Ward showed him the small place on the button that hadn't been there before he'd left for Texas. "I know I can have the thing replaced, but I'm ready for a new one anyway."

Bill dropped before him and inspected the button. On his hands and knees like this Ward felt his belly tighten and his cock swell. He was just reaching out to pull Bill to his lengthening cock when the phone rang at the desk. Ward took a step back.

What the fuck was he doing? When Bill rubbed his hand over his own cock and smiled up at Ward, fear and anger nearly took him to his knees. Taking another step back, Ward reached out for something to hold onto when his hands curled around a sign just as Bill cupped his balls.

A surge of something so powerful made him swing out with the sign. Ward had no idea what came over him, but thoughts of Bill sucking his cock made him both aroused and pissed. Anger won over.

Ward had no idea what had happened when he sort of stepped back into himself. There was blood all over him, as well as the rack of clothes in front of him. Feet stuck out from under the clothes that dripped blood, and Ward was almost afraid to look at the rest of the body. Dropping the sign, he looked around.

"Mother fuck." Ward raced to the front of the store and locked it. He turned over the closed sign and turned off the lights. Backing away, he tried to think what the hell he was supposed to do now. When he realized his prints were everywhere, he grabbed a shirt off another rack and started wiping things down he knew he'd touched. The door, the lock, and anything else he might have brushed against. When he was sure he had gotten everything but the sign, he looked down at his own clothing.

"Look what you did," Ward screamed at the legs. "You've ruined my only nice suit with your...your touching. Now what the fuck am I going to do? I can't go see my brother like this."

He was panicking. Ward took deep breaths trying to calm himself. He'd been in a situation like this before and knew that things had to be done. Cameras. He looked around all the walls and saw three of them. If he remembered correctly that was what had nearly gotten him caught once before. Going to the back room, he found a messy office and tore through it looking for something that would be used for recording. That's when he decided that they were fake. There was nothing in the entire room to indicate that anything had recorded what had happened. Looking down at his clothes again, Ward realized he'd have to have something to wear. Going back out onto the sales floor, he nearly screamed when he heard someone knocking at the locked door.

Holding his breath, Ward wondered if someone else might have a key and could let themselves in, but the person moved away. Going to the rack he'd first been looking at, he found himself a suit that would more than likely fit him and took it to the changing room to see.

He'd had to make three trips to find something suitable. What the hell these people were thinking when they put the jackets on one side of the room and the pants on the other was beyond him. When he finally had what he wanted, he went to the back again and stripped down. There was no way he was going to be all bloodied, so he washed as best he could, using the wipes he found while looking for a recorder. Ward finally had to sit down and rest.

"Why am I rushing around as if there is a closing time I have to worry about?" The sound of his own voice calmed him somewhat, and he went to the little refrigerator and found, much to his surprise, a thick roast beef sandwich from a deli he'd only heard of and several colas. He was finishing off the cheesecake he'd also found when he thought of the cash register.

Finally, he thought. *Something is going my way.* There was nearly four grand in the drawer, as well as five hundred he'd found in Bills pants. In the open safe that he'd noticed earlier, he found an additional ten thousand dollars and several credit card receipts.

Ward had had some minor luck with a few stolen credit cards in his day. Mostly, it was the people he'd been staying with and it was that that had gotten him kicked out of a couple of the places he'd been living at. Smiling, he wrote down all the numbers as well as the security code that had been provided for him. Calling the airport, he bought himself a round trip ticket to Ohio as well as booked a hotel for when he got there. He was all set. Now he needed some things to wear.

Two hours later he was dressed and had packed him a lovely suitcase with all the things he'd ever need. The clothing shop had a great selection and he was able not only to get himself outfitted in pants and shirts, but also expensive underwear and tee-shirts all made of hand-spun silk. Ward locked up with the keys he'd found on the counter.

Ward stood outside the back of the shop, trying to remember if he'd cleaned everything up. He'd wiped things down three times as well as used the wipes again on Bill's face and hands. Ward wasn't sure if he'd actually touched him, but he wasn't taking any chances. When he was on the main street again, he flagged down a cab and was on his way to the airport when he realized he should have taken Bill's phone too. Damn it all to hell and back, he thought he'd gotten everything. Oh well, no hope for it.

Smiling as he leaned back his head, Ward was thinking about the reunion that he and Thad were going to have. He knew now that his brother had no idea he'd been coming to see him, and if

Ward could find Morton he'd show him just how he dealt with liars. But dead was dead and he was sure that Morton was as dead as old Bill was. Pulling out his brand new wallet, he paid the driver too much and told him to keep the change. He was flush now, and Ward was going to make sure everyone knew who they were dealing with. Ward Galloway was back, and he was fucking taking names and kicking some major ass.

~~~

Thad was just putting his phone away when it vibrated in his hand. He saw that it was Jane and wondered briefly if the bank had notified her and got up to leave the bedroom so he could talk to her.

"You're not going to believe what your brother has done," she said in way of greeting. "He's wanted for robbery as well as murder."

"What happened?" Thad had since gotten rid of Robert after making an offer on the house. Diamond lay on the big bed after they'd had sex, and slept all covered up in his suit coat. He didn't want to wake her just yet, knowing that she'd be embarrassed when she did. He, however, could have shouted to the world that he'd rendered her unconscious.

"Apparently he entered a clothing store at about ten this morning and was looking at suits. Three hours later he's gone and the proprietor is dead, his head beaten in with a sign." Thad leaned back against the wall as she continued. "According to my friend on the force, it looks like Ward was about to get his pipes cleaned up by William Bolsterer when for some reason Ward decided he wasn't interested. I guess simply saying no was out of the question. Actually, I didn't even know your brother was a homosexual."

"He's not, not that I'm aware of. Not that it matters." Thad looked up when Diamond sat up on the bed. He watched her reach for her clothes that he'd picked up for her and was completely distracted by her so much that Jane's laughter was all that brought him back.

"Where did you go? Some woman I'm hoping." She laughed harder. He decided to let her know what was going on.

"It is, as a matter of fact. Diamond Erickson and I have just purchased a house here and we're going to be moving in as soon as it's cleaned from top to bottom." That shut her up. When Diamond came into the bathroom with him, he pulled her hips back to his groin when she leaned over to get a drink. Her soft moan had his cock aching to take her again.

"That's good news, but if you think I'm going to run this place with you up there, you're nuts. I'll hunt you down and drain you if you even think of it." He hadn't thought of anything other than being close to Diamond and her family since they'd had sex.

"There's an opening here if you want it, but you have to find your replacement before—"

"Done. I've been training someone for my vacation anyway, and I'll step up the training. Where am I moving to anyway?" He told her. "Okay, I'll have to find somewhere to stay until…Christ, did you say Ohio?"

"Yes. It's a nice little town and you'll love it." Diamond turned to look at him as he continued talking to Jane. "You will be notified by the bank up here, a man by the name of Robert Beck. He's going to verify that I have the funds to purchase mine and Diamond's little house."

Diamond snorted at him, and he pulled her closer to his body. Jane laughed. "Little, huh? You don't strike me as a little bugaboo sort of guy."

"It's not. But Diamond loves it, and I want her to have it. Make sure that happens for me too." He knew that she'd understand that he wanted the house in her name, and when she asked about her middle initial, he had to ask Diamond what it was.

"It's Ava. Why?" Thad kissed her nose and relayed the information to Jane. After asking her to let him know when she found out anything about Ward, he hung up.

"I've bought the house, or we have. As of an hour ago." Thad watched her absorb this information before he continued. "I don't want you to be upset, but the house will be in your name as owner."

"I can't afford this thing." He smiled. "What happens if you decide you no longer want me, or worse yet, you decide this little town isn't what you had in mind? I could never pay the bills on this thing, much less the mortgage."

"The house will be paid in full, and as for me leaving you, that's not going to happen either." He took her hand and they descended the stairs to what he had hoped would be his office. After she was seated, he sat as well. "I know you have no reason to believe or trust me, but I want you to try, for me; no, I guess I want you to try for us."

Thad watched her closely. She was processing and he loved that about her. Emptying her head out to work out a problem wasn't something that she did. He could almost see her making a long list of things she wanted to say and going through each one of them and tweaking it, marking it off if she found the answers.

When she looked up at him Thad realized two things at once. One, he was in love with her. Not the sort of staggering love that he knew that Blair and Sapphire had, but a gentle I-need-you-to-function love. It wasn't that he didn't think they'd get to the I-fucking-can't-live-without-you love, but for now, this was enough.

And second, Thad realized he wasn't going to be bored again. Smiling, he waited for her to begin because he had no doubt she would soon enough. When she looked at him, he saw the tears sprinkled in her lashes and felt his heart take a tight twist. Maybe he was wrong about the kind of love he was in; he thought he had fallen right into the "can't live" one.

"I know you have a great deal of money…that's not true. I know you have money, but the amount is just too staggering to take in right now, so I'm leaving it at that. But I don't know how to be the kind of person you need." When he started to ask her what she meant, she continued. "You need a woman who can be in the background. The kind that would look beautiful on your arm and smile at the kind of people I hate. I don't know how to run a house the size of the one my family lives in, much less the one you bought. How am I supposed to keep up with it? And there's the pool and the—"

Thad got up and went to her, kneeling before her as she sobbed quietly. Lifting her chin up, he looked into her eyes and found that he was a goner. This was the woman he was going to spend the rest of his life not only loving, but worshiping as well. Smiling at her, he brushed away her tears with his thumb.

"I have a staff. Not nearly large enough for this house, but one that can run this one as well as the two of us. I've already called Benson. He's the head of the house in Texas. I told him what I needed. He'll be calling you in a couple of days." Thad didn't know if now was the time or not, but he decided that she might as well know it all. "I've asked Jane to set up your name on all my accounts, personal as well as business. You won't be able to make any decisions with the business without some more experience, but you'll be able to do that soon I'm sure. I've also had her order you a cell phone. I noticed that while you have one, it's out of date and I want to be able to reach you when I need to just hear your voice."

"You're leaving, aren't you?" He nodded. "I guess I assumed you would but I didn't…how long will you be gone?"

Thad was thrilled to no end that she knew he was returning. "I'll have to leave today. I'm sorry but I have to…I have a brother. His name is Ward. He's murdered someone and I have to go down and see what kind of mess he's left behind for me to clean up."

"Murdered? You're not going to pay people off, are you?" He was shocked, but then realized that had been what he'd first thought, too, when Jane had told him. "I won't stand for you using your money to make a murderer go free."

"He won't. Ward is a pain in my ass, and according to Jane, the murder was brutal and he is on the run. I don't know if he'll come here or not, but I've already made some arrangements for security to come here and set up the house. The cleaning crew will be here in the morning."

"You work fast." He nodded at her and smiled. "I thought there was some sort of waiting period or something. But I guess if you have enough money, things sort of happen fast."

"Something like that." He reached into his pocket, then took her hand. "I know that this is going to be fast as well, but I was wondering if you'd marry me."

"Oh my." Thad moved the ring over her knuckles to set it home. "You do work fast. This is...Thad, this is beautiful."

"Is that a yes?" Smiling, she nodded and Thad felt his life settle. Diamond Erickson was going to be his wife.

Chapter 12

Sapphire walked into the kitchen to grab a glass of tea before she headed to her home office. Grandmother was standing at the stove staring at Diamond, who looked like she was deep in thought. Sapphire looked at her grandmother.

"I don't know what's wrong with her. I came in just to start on dinner and she was sitting there staring at that glass like it was going to give her the secrets of life. And don't even bother speaking to her. She's not uttered a single word." Grandmother huffed as she continued. "And Thad left too. I got this off the table."

Sapphire took the note and read it quickly. *I'll be back before you know it. Do all the things we discussed and don't forget to call me if you have any problems. Love, Thad.*

Jade and Ruby came in just as Sapphire sat across from Diamond. Each of them sat down when Grandmother told them what was going on. Diamond continued to sit very still as Emerald walked in.

"What's up?" Grandmother explained to Emerald what she'd just told the other two. "So she's upset that he's left her already? What an idiotic turd head."

"Who's an idiotic turd head? And where do you get those names you call people," Opal asked as she entered the melee. "I swear you just reach out and grab a couple of words and mash them together."

"I do. And it's Diamond. She's in a trance or something because lover-boy has left her and she's more than likely knocked up and will resort to drugs when—" Sapphire cut Emerald off.

"Do you mind not making up stories right now? This is serious. I think she's depressed." Sapphire was just reaching for her phone to call Thad and give him a piece of her mind when Diamond spoke.

"I have a house now. A great big one. I have to go and buy things for it. There's furniture but no sheets and towels for us to use. Benson will be here on Friday, but he will be busy hiring a staff." Diamond laid a credit card on the table, and that's when Sapphire saw the ring. "I'm to use that to do it all."

Emerald grabbed Diamond's hand and whistled. "Good Christ, did he rob a bank while he was at it? This is the most beautiful ring I've ever seen. I guess he popped the question."

"He did. And I said yes, but now I'm...you want to go shopping with me?" Diamond looked at them all. "I could take you to the house to show you around. Then you can help me get whatever we're going to need."

There was a great deal of desperation there and Sapphire had a feeling they all heard it and not just her. She did pull out her cell then and contacted her office while she noticed the rest of them were making arrangements as well. When Allen, Blair's dad, walked in the kitchen, he was absorbed in the shopping spree as well. Before any of them had a chance to ask any more questions, a large man in a black suit knocked on the back door.

"Miss Erickson?" They all nodded, confusing the man. "Diamond Erickson? My name is Jon, and I'm going to be your driver and security guard today. Mr. Galloway asked that someone be with you at all times."

He handed Diamond an envelope and stood very still while he waited for her to read it. When Diamond handed it to her, she laughed at what was there.

I know you can more than likely kill anything that dares to come at you with ill intent, but for my own peace of mind, could you please allow Jon to hang around with you today? Also, take your sisters and grandmother with you today and have them help you. And don't be overwhelmed again. You're going to be fine. Love, T.

"I guess we're all going shopping." As they all piled into the extra-long Hummer, Diamond looked as nervous as Sapphire'd ever seen her. Sapphire wasn't sure if it was the house or the fact that Thad was going to be gone for a few days. Allen helped them figure it out.

"Heard tell you got this house big enough for ten families to live in. You gonna fill it with some grandkids for your grandmother or you gonna be selfish like this one is being?" Sapphire flushed, not wanting to mention to anyone that she thought she was pregnant just yet. "I've been waiting my whole life for a grandson and haven't gotten a single one to show for it."

"I don't know." Diamond smiled at Allen as she continued. "I really don't want kids, and I'm pretty sure Thad doesn't either. Sapphire and Blair told me that they were never having babies. They're too messy."

Allen's mouth opened and closed several times before he glared at Diamond. When she laughed, he glared harder.

"You, young lady, are not funny. To tease an old man like that about his legacy? That's shameful." Allen crossed his arms over his chest and looked at her. "I suppose I'll have to wait until next season for a baby to hold from you as well."

"I'm not sure. We'll let you know when we know." Allen huffed at her. "You should know that I do plan to tell my husband before I do you anyway."

The house, if one could call it simply a house, was much bigger than she'd imagined. Blair had told her how many square feet it was, but this…this was amazing. The front entrance alone was breathtaking, but the deeper they got into the house, the more Sapphire could see why her sister was overwhelmed. And the pool was something she could see herself using if they had one.

"You'll come over all the time, right? And bring bread crumbs?" She and Diamond were in the master suite taking an inventory of what was needed in there. The list wasn't as long as it could have been, but they were still finding things the young couple would need.

"I'd say bread crumbs would be a good start. You'll need a great deal of help to keep this place just dusted." Diamond nodded as she moved to the large window near the gas fireplace. "Diamond, tell me what's wrong."

"I don't know how to be rich." Sapphire started to laugh, but when her sister continued, she was glad that she hadn't. "I mean look at this place. How on earth am I going to ever feel comfortable here?"

Sapphire thought she already did but didn't comment on that. "What makes you feel like this? The house or the man?"

"He doesn't love me." Sapphire sat next to her on the bed. "He said he liked me a few days ago, but he gave me this house because I liked it. Who gives someone a house because they liked it?"

"Men." Diamond laughed as Sapphire continued. "You have to realize that they only know how to fix things either by manly means or buying new. I don't know if Thad doesn't love you or not. If he doesn't, he's very close. Do you love him?"

"Yes." Diamond got up to go to the closet as she finished telling her what was bothering her the most. "What if I embarrass him at some function?"

"Embarrass him how? By saying the wrong thing? Telling someone to kiss your ass? I'm pretty sure he knows you well enough by now to realize you're not the sit back sort of woman."

"I told him that too, and he told me he wanted me to be that way. What will happen if I say that to some dick who's making me want to shift and tear out his throat?" Diamond turned back to her as she spoke. "I don't want to lose him."

"You won't. And if you tear out someone's throat, I'll help you bury the body." Diamond hugged her. "I love you very much. I want you to be happy here. Will you be?"

"Yes. I love this house. I know it's huge and I'll get lost in it a lot at first, but I really do love it. We're going to have so much fun here." She moved to the bathroom before she continued. "But we need to get some towels in here or no one will have a good time."

Three hours later, after a huge lunch at Diamond's favorite restaurant, they were hitting the mall. In pairs, they emptied the shelves. By dinnertime, not only were they exhausted, but had enough stuff purchased that they had to make arrangements to have a truck brought and loaded. Thad was going to be either completely surprised or one pissed off man. Sapphire thought he was going to be amazed rather than anything else.

~~~

Ward wasn't happy. The airport wouldn't give him a car without a valid driver's license, and when he'd asked where his brother was staying, the woman at the information desk had simply walked away.

It wasn't like he thought the desk had all the information he needed, but his brother was the biggest thing these people would ever see, and Ward could not understand why they didn't care who he was either. She'd looked at him like he was a blot on a wall when he'd explained to her twice who he was. Nothing, not even a little bit of recognition. Stupid cow. Ward ended up having to take a cab to his hotel, and that, too, had been a complete let down.

No limo service was available to him. Not even being Ward Galloway had impressed them enough to call someone in to do it. How was that even possible? Didn't these Podunk people know to have one in reserve for rich people like him?

Ward was checking into the hotel when he saw a newspaper lying on the counter. He snatched it up so quickly he knocked several copies to the floor. When the clerk at the counter came to pick them up, he stopped her by putting his foot on the copies.

"Is this true?" Ward pointed to the headline. "This says that my brother bought a house here. Why the hell would they print a lie like this and think to get away with it? He'd no more live in this nasty town than I would."

"You are not a nice person, are you?" She stood up and took the paper from him. "No, it's not true. We have the paper lie for us every day so that we can watch the reaction of people on a daily basis. It's a lifelong goal of mine to make someone have a heart attack one of these days."

He wasn't amused and nearly told her so when he looked into her face. She was scary. Her name tag said her name was Diane and that she was with guest relations. Well, not when his brother found out about her.

It took Ward an hour to find out where his brother's new house was. It might have taken him less time had he been able to get any of the hotel staff to help him, but every time he called down to the desk, he was either put on hold for a long time or hung up on. He'd finally had to read the entire article himself, which had listed the address right on the page. Ward decided it was time to pay his brother a little visit.

The cab ride took nearly forty minutes, and through the most run down parts of town. He supposed these people didn't see it like he did, as he had the eyes of the rich and famous, but none of the houses were up to his standards and Ward wondered, not for the first time, what the hell his brother was thinking.

There were several vans in front of the mansion as well as a few pick-up trucks with the name of a security firm on them. Now this was a house he could live in and vowed that he would. Ward decided that he'd move in now if it had any staff in it. He walked up on the front stairs and started to enter, but was blocked by a man that looked like he lifted trucks for fun.

"You don't belong here." Ward nodded at him and reached for his wallet. "Unless you want me to rip your arm from its socket, you'd better just stand the fuck still."

What scared Ward the most about the man's threat was that, first of all, it wasn't one. A threat implied that he might do it. He had a feeling this man would do it with pleasure. And secondly, the way it had been delivered. No hard voice or even all that much inflection in his voice. He could have been telling Ward that it was going to snow in an hour. But there was no doubt that the man could and would do what he said.

"I was going to show you my identification." The man nodded, but Ward still didn't reach again for it. "I'm...my brother owns this house. He'd tell you if you'll call him out."

"You're not going in unless someone tells me you can, and if Mr. Galloway is your brother, he didn't mention it to me. His wife didn't either." Before Ward could tell the burly man that Thad wasn't married, he corrected himself. "Future wife I mean. And Miss Erickson didn't say a single word about you showing up either."

"My brother is not engaged." The man didn't say anything to him. "I would know if he was engaged, and our kind does not marry women from Ohio. We marry princesses from other countries and actresses. We do not marry below our station."

The man shoved him in the chest and Ward went flying off the front stairs. He might have tumbled over a few more times but he hit one of the other men who'd been going in and out of the house without anyone stopping him. Ward started to stand up but decided the view was better from there, and the man standing over him didn't look as if he was going to let him stand up anyway.

"You get yourself back into your little car there and tell that driver to haul your skinny little ass back to wherever it is you hatched from. We folks from Ohio don't care for your kind either, and just as soon you didn't fuck with our pretty little women who, by the way, could eat you for dinner and never break a sweat."

Ward reached into his pocket and pulled out his notepad. He'd been keeping notes on his phone, but since someone had shut it off, he had to resort to keeping his lists this way. He glanced up at the man

"What is your name? As soon as my brother hears about this, he's going to be pissed. And when he finds out who you are, he's going to have you fired." He was ready for the man to beg him for forgiveness, but when the man snorted, Ward looked up at him.

"You think I'm afraid of you?" He moved down to Ward's level, yet still managed to tower over him. "Samuel Mac Tire is my name, and in the event you don't know, that's Irish for wolf."

Ward moved back from the man as far as he possibly could when he sort of...shifted. Gone was the huge burly man with dark eyes, and in his place was a snarling fucking huge wolf.

When he moved close enough that Ward could feel his hot breath in his face, for the second time in his life, he pissed himself. And if he didn't know better, he would have thought the wolf was laughing at him. Ward looked up when the shadow that seemed to be over him disappeared. Now an entirely different man stood over him.

"Sam said you were to get the fuck out of here and not return so long as we're here. I'd listen if I was you. Alpha left him in charge, and he ain't gonna be none too happy when he finds out you was here fucking with his foreman." Ward struggled to stand and the man snickered at Wards pants front. "Got you a little scared, did he? He's good at that. Sam is my sister's mate, but he scares me too. She calls him a teddy bear, but me? I don't think so."

"I'll sue for this." The man nodded. "When I'm finished, I'll own this company and you're all going to be sorry."

"I don't think you're gonna have much luck with that there, buddy, but you go right on ahead and try." He looked around before he smiled at him. "You try and fuck with this company and you'll never see the light of day again."

Ward was on his way back to his hotel, not remembering how he'd gotten into the taxi but how he'd gotten the tear in his suit. Not that he planned on keeping it. After all, the man had soiled it for him. Ward looked down at his stained pants and tried to reason how someone had gotten the drop on him and peed down his front.

Things were not going well for him, and he wanted to talk to his brother. When he was back at his hotel, the lady at the desk said his name, but he was in a hurry to get to his room and take a long, hot shower. When someone tapped him on the shoulder, he turned to snarl at them, but saw it was the lady from the desk.

"This came for you," she said. He nearly dropped the package she'd shoved in his chest. "There is no need for you to sign for it, and I'm pretty sure you weren't going to tip the guy, so I did both."

Before he could tell her she was stupid if she thought he was going to tell her thanks, she was gone. This was the rudest bunch of people he'd ever met. And to think he'd been about to stay another few days.

He opened the envelope on the top of the package and read the letter.

When you get this call me, a cell phone to reach me has already been programmed in. And the phone only has two hours of minutes on it so don't think you can call your friends...if you have any left. I'm in no mood to piss around about this, Ward, so don't fucking put it off. Thad Galloway.

Ward waited until he got to his room before he opened the package itself. The nerve of his brother treating him this way was beyond what he deserved. Had Thad simply been where he should have been, they could have had this settled days ago. After his shower, he sat down and took out the cheap phone.

It didn't even have a camera on it. And the flip type opening had him snarl at it. What was wrong with a nice expensive one? he wondered. It wasn't like Thad couldn't have afforded it. Hell, he thought, he could have owned the company if he wanted. It might be something Ward could talk him into when they were back at the office.

The phone was answered on the first ring. "What the fuck are you thinking? Or are you?" Before he could answer Thad, he continued. "I come to Texas to see what mess you've gotten yourself into only to find that you've taken off to God knows where to get into something deeper. I'm fucking not bailing your ass out of this one."

"What are you talking about? And I don't appreciate the tone you're using right now. Take a deep breath and tell me what mess you think I've gotten myself into."

Silence. All Ward could hear was his own breath. Looking at the phone, he wasn't surprised to see it still counting the seconds for the call. Thad could be terrifying when he was quiet like this.

"You murdered a man. In cold blood, and then had the fucking nerve to rob him too." Ward felt his heart pound in his chest. How did he know? How had they found out he'd done it? "Stay put. I'm coming home and will be there in five hours."

Ward closed the phone and hopped up. There was no fucking way he was going to wait for his brother to come and find him. He was going to be long gone before that happened. Slipping the phone in his pocket, he went to the bedroom to pack. He was out of there right now.

Chapter 13

Thad's plane landed at close to midnight. He was exhausted and wanted nothing more than to go to bed and sleep for an entire week. As soon as he entered the quiet terminal, he felt the weight of the past five days leave his body. Reaching for his bag, he was startled to find someone take it from him.

"You look like you could use a good soak in a tub." He stared at Diamond for a full ten seconds before she spoke again. "Did you forget me while you were gone?"

"Hell no." Dropping everything he had in his hands, he pulled her to him and kissed her. She tasted of honey that she drank in her tea, as well as sex. He pulled from her mouth with a great deal of reluctance, but didn't let go of her. "I should have taken you with me. I'm sure I would have felt a great deal better."

"But I wouldn't have been able to get the house ready for you. Benson said that—" He kissed her again, cutting her off.

Only just managing to lift his head long enough to look down at her, he smiled. Christ, he was so in love with her. Taking her hand, he grabbed up his suitcase and carry-on and walked to the front of the airport. A car was waiting for him, and so was his driver Patterson.

"Welcome home, sir. I've managed to get the garage ready for the two cars you've stated that you wanted brought here, and the others...they have arrived as well." Thad nodded as he slipped inside. He had ordered Diamond a car from Texas in the middle of the night two nights ago. They'd been talking on the phone and she'd told him how her car was in for repairs. The new one was to be delivered sometime that day.

As soon as the car was in motion, he pulled her over his lap. It had been five days without her, and he was more than a little needy. When she reached for his tie and pulled it off him, Thad thought he could get used to this, but stilled her hands.

"I've bought you something." Her eyes were glazed with need, and he was ready to give her just about anything she wanted when he thought about the gifts. "I want to put them on you now."

"Now?" He nodded, reached for the hem of her shirt, and pulled it up, only to be stopped by her grabbing it. "We're in a car. Moving down the road. What are you going to do to me?"

The clamps had nearly gotten him tossed off the plane, but the woman who had searched him when the alarm sounded must have had a working knowledge of what they were, because she told him to put them in his pocket and to have fun. He'd been as hard as a rock since she'd waved him through.

"They're going to make what I have planned for you so much more delicious." He showed them to her and felt her body rock over his. "Lift your shirt for me."

She did so without hesitation this time. And when he ordered her to remove her bra, she did that as well. Christ, he wasn't sure what he'd been thinking, but having her pert nipple so close to his mouth, he nearly said fuck the clamps and tossed her back onto the seat.

Pinching her nipple hard, he rocked up into her when she moaned. "I'm going to suck your nipple hard, and then I'm going to put these on you. You'll have to let me know when it's too tight."

Her nod had him pulling her as close as he could get her and nipping at her hard nub. Suckling hard, he tried to think what he wanted to do to her first when he got her home. He knew that the equipment had been delivered and set up yesterday, but he'd made her promise not to go into the room until he got there. Lifting his head, he watched as her once pink flesh turned a deep red, almost purple. Slipping the ring over the tip, he started to twist down the clamp.

"Did you peak into the room?" Her moan made his cock jerk in his trousers, but she didn't tell him to stop. "Slave?"

"No, master. I didn't peak in the room. But they assured me everything was...too much."

He stopped immediately and licked the blood-filled tip. When he blew over the clamp, she curled her fingers into his shoulder and threw back her head. Thad took the other offered breast to his mouth and gave it the same treatment. She was breathing as hard as he was when he finished.

"Does it hurt?" She nodded, then shook her head. "Good. We need to have a safe word. Did you think of one yet?"

He'd told her what it was for, the safe word, and asked her to pick one she could easily remember and say if she needed him to stop. He'd been surprised when she told him that she'd learned about the colors as well. He had a feeling she was going to be the best sub he'd ever had.

"Clouds. I'm going to use clouds." He nodded and set her off him and onto the seat next to him.

"How long do we have before we get to the house?" She told him forty minutes. "Good. I want you to suck my cock until we get there."

He leaned back on the seat and opened his pants. It wasn't what he really wanted and that was to be buried deep inside of her, but he needed the edge taken off and knew that she could probably use it too.

As soon as he freed his cock, he watched her face as she stared at him. He fisted his cock and stroked it twice before he told her to take him. As soon as her mouth covered him, he nearly came up off the seat. She was as hot as any flame he'd ever been near and more talented with her tongue than he could ever imagine.

Adjusting her on the seat, he lifted her pretty little skirt up so that he could feel her ass. Tearing the panty away, he smacked her hard and felt her nip at his cock from the surprise.

"Next time you and I are alone and you have on a skirt, I want you to not wear panties. If I want to fuck you, I don't want to have to wait for you to be naked." She moaned around his cock, and he slapped her again. "What did I warn you about?"

"Yes, master, when I wear a skirt, I'm to wear no panties. You want to fuck me, you want me ready." Sliding his fingers down the seam of her ass, he could feel she was already ready. Slick wetness covered his fingers.

He watched her suck him until he was dizzy with the need to come. Slapping her ass twice more, he buried his fingers deep inside of her, careful not to touch her clit. She was going to pay for a little while, and that would mean no climax. Soaking the tight bud at her ass, she tensed around him.

"Don't do that. I won't hurt you." He moved the lubricant all over her tight muscles until she began to roll with him. Pressing his finger inside of her had him nearly cry out when she bit him. "Careful, love, or we'll be finished before we begin."

Sweat trickled down his arms as he slowly moved in and out of her. When she was ready, he pressed a second finger in her and then after a bit, a third.

"I'm going to fuck you here when you're stretched out for me." He scissored his fingers as she licked the length of him twice. "Then I'm going to fuck that pretty pussy of yours with a fat vibrator until your need to come is nearly ready to kill you."

She sucked his head into her mouth so hard that he pushed hard into her ass, momentarily forgetting she wasn't used to it. Thad felt his balls tighten to his body and wrapped his hands into her hair with his free hand.

"Swallow me." Her gagging reflex nearly had him come, but when she swallowed his cock down, he felt his body ready. Slamming his fingers in and out of her as fast as he could, he rolled his hips up into her awaiting mouth until he knew he was going to come. As soon as she moaned around him, the vibration moved along his cock and straight to his balls. Thad cried out as he emptied himself down the back of her throat.

He had to fuck her. Thad nearly threw her to the floor, grabbing her and flipping her over. His cock was thickening, and as soon as she spread her legs for him, he pulled her over him and down over his cock. Diamond nuzzled his neck, and he knew that the moment her teeth broke skin he was going to come. Holding her to him, he closed his eyes when she licked him, and as soon as her teeth sank into him, Thad shouted out her name and commanded her to come with him.

Thad had no idea if she did or not. His own climax was building again until he was sure he was going to die from it. When she leaned back, cupping her breasts, he took her nipple, clamp and all, into his mouth and bit her. His third climax in as few as ten minutes was too much. And before he could try to think what the hell was happening to him, he felt his world black out.

Diamond hated to wake him, but they were nearly home. Her body ached for more from him, but he'd only told her to come the one time, and she wasn't going to think that just because he'd brought her as close to the edge as she thought possible without falling over, he'd only said the one time. And she was going to be the best sub she could be. Thad blinked at her several times before he smiled.

"We're nearly home." He reached for her, and she backed up, but only slightly. "As much as I'd like to have you fuck me again, I'm afraid there just isn't nearly enough time. Master."

"I'm going to eat you when we get in the bedroom." She nearly told him fuck it and begged him to do it now. The car would just have to be stopped for a little while longer. "Did you come?"

"Yes, master." He asked her if she was sated. "No, master. I need...I would be happy if you could give me more."

"I plan on it. Much more. But you won't come tonight. Not unless I'm feeling very generous." He fixed his pants as he continued. "Do you have any idea how much I want to fuck you again right now?"

"Yes, master." He glanced at her as she put his belt back to rights. "Will it be all right if I ready myself to exit the car?"

He nodded. "As soon as we are in the house, I want you to go to our bedroom and strip down. I will meet you there when I'm ready for you. Stand near the door to our playroom and be naked."

Her body felt the implication of his words all the way to her toes. He was going to play with her, and she almost couldn't wait. Diamond had to take several deep breaths before she could answer him.

"I will go to the play room and wait for your command. I will be naked and ready for you until you arrive." He nodded and turned to watch her as she put her shirt back on. Her nipples were simply too tender for her bra, but he held out his hand for it and slipped it into his pocket as she pulled her shirt over her head. Even the soft cotton was making her ache.

They didn't speak again. She wasn't sure she could have said anything to him other than to beg him to take her, and he seemed to be more interested in the small pad he'd had in his briefcase. Diamond's body was throbbing with need.

When the car slid to a stop, she moved to get out when he pulled her to him. Thad looked at her face so intently that she was afraid for a few minutes. He kissed her gently on the mouth before he put his forehead to hers.

"I've not hurt you, have I?" She shook her head. "I…you can't believe how much you've pleased me right now. All I can think about and have thought about is watching you while I take my whip to your luscious ass."

The thoughts of what he was saying no longer scared her. Squirming slightly on the seat, she opened her legs just a little for him. She wasn't sure he could smell her or not, but when he moaned, she knew that he could even just a little.

"Go. Go now before I change my mind and take you right here." His harsh laugh made her look at him. "You'd think for as much as you drained me I'd be able to take my time. But all I want to do is lay you over this seat and suckle at your clit until you can't walk."

Diamond didn't run, no matter how much she really wanted to. But she did skip down along the hallway when she was out of sight. She had no idea what was on the other side of the door off from their bedroom, but she couldn't wait to find out. He walked in the door as she was just getting to the door.

"Come here. I want you to undress me. But don't touch me." She moved slowly forward to do as he bid. "When I'm done, I'm going to take a shower and you're going to bathe me."

Diamond wasn't sure her pussy could have gotten any wetter, but she could feel her juices as they moved down her leg. When she pulled his jacket off, she laid it over the chair and tried to figure out how to do this.

"My tie next." She wanted to thank him for helping her but reached for his silk tie first. "I will need to go to Texas again in a few weeks, and I'd like for you to go with me. I know that you have to work, but I need your help down there."

"Doing what?" She flushed, not knowing if this was a master/slave thing. "I'm not very good at this just yet."

"You're doing fine. Because we have a house there that needs to be sold, and I'd like for you to see if there's anything in the house that you'd like. Some of the things were my mother's, but my father's things…they're all gone."

She stilled and looked at him. "You didn't care for him? And whatever was your mother's, I'll take. I may not have any rights to it as your wife, but if we have children, they should at least see it."

"You have every right to it and more. And no, my father and I never got along. He is the one that spoiled Ward to the point where he thinks everything is owed to him. Then when he died, Ward seemed to think that the world owed him everything. I tried to work with him, to get him on the straight path, but…." He moved out of her reach. "He killed a man back home. Murdered him, stole his money as well as what was in the register, and even had the nerve to steal his suits. He's here in Ohio now, Ward is. I'm not sure…."

"We'll take care of this." Diamond moved to stand in front of him as she unbuttoned his shirt. "There are a great many things we can do as a pack that humans can't. Like, for instance, we can move in and out of areas that a human…most humans…won't. And do things that no sane person would be able to do."

"Like?" She stepped behind him to take off his shirt and forgot about the cufflinks. She had to work at them while she tried to think how to answer his question.

"Like wooded forest where there is no light. We can see much better than they would be able to. We can also sniff out our prey when all a human has to rely on is their own, lesser ability." Diamond didn't want to tell him all of it, but when he put his hands on her bare arms and held her, she couldn't keep it from him.

"We can kill without thought. Our kind can murder in ways that would sicken most people; our prey would be no more. I don't mean they would be dead, I'm saying that no trace of them would ever be found by any means." She looked Thad in the eye as she finished. "I can kill him and you'd never know it but for my confession."

Neither of them said anything for several seconds. She wanted to step back and leave him, knowing that he was going to ask her questions. Diamond didn't want to answer them, but if he asked, she'd have no choice.

"How did he hurt you?" She was more startled by the question than she could believe. When she started to pull away from him, he pulled her back and held her still. "How?"

"It was the night that Jeffery Benetton tried to hurt Sapphire. A man, one of his enforcers, was dragging us out of the house when he suddenly stopped. Harris, Jeffery's brother, had gone ahead with my sisters, but Derek decided to…." Diamond moved away, and he let her this time, so she pulled his shirt over her nakedness. "He was going to kill me, after he raped me. He told me that…he said that I was going to bleed out while he fucked me."

She moved to the window that was nearest the fireplace, and despite the warmth outside, she was suddenly cold all the way to her bones. Closing her eyes, she thought of him dragging her to the shed just out from the house.

"Derek said I was his prize. He said that Jeffery had told him he could have his pick and I was his for the night. He'd hit me before, so I was stunned a little, but as soon as we got to the shed and he locked us in, I started to feel a little less out of it." She remembered his breath on her throat and his body, soft and smelling of sweat as he slammed her against the wall. "I didn't have a choice, and my wolf knew it. It was him or me. She took me and…and she killed him in cold blood."

"He would have killed you if you hadn't." She shook her head, not looking at Thad as he spoke. "Do you think that you did something wrong?"

"I took his life." Thad wrapped his arms around her waist and held her back to his chest. "His family never knew what happened to him, never found a trace of him to this day. I've lived with this since that night."

"Thank you." She looked at him over her shoulder. "You killing him saved me. Had you not, then I would have come along, me this puny little human, and died protecting your honor. You killed him to be with me."

Diamond laughed, which she supposed he meant for her to do. "I murdered someone and got away with it." She nodded when he shook his head. "I did. You can't think that what I did was right."

"Of course I do. I told you, had you not killed him, he would most assuredly have killed you. And there is no way of knowing how many others he would have killed after you." He kissed her gently on the mouth. "You are an amazing woman, have I told you that?"

"No. And I doubt very much I believe you now." She turned in his arms. "I guess I sort of ruined the mood."

"No. You just changed it a little." He kissed her again. "Come on, I want to show you our play room. But next time, you're going to undress me completely or I'll punish you."

The door had been closed all afternoon to her. She'd been tempted to sneak a peek and see what he had put in there, but the thought of him showing her was what she really wanted. When he kicked off his shoes but left his pants in place she felt a shiver of anticipation run over her body. Even her wolf was excited.

He opened the door with a flourish, and she stepped in when he waved her through. Diamond had been looking up what kind of equipment he might buy, but nothing prepared her for what he'd done to the little room. She turned to look at him when he moved close to her.

"Welcome to our playroom." She nodded. "Now take off your clothes and go over to that hump. It's time for me to beat your ass."

.

Chapter 14

Thad wanted to watch her explore the room, but she'd been through an emotional set back and he wanted to make her think of something else. As she dropped his shirt to the floor and made her way over to the hump, he moved to the cabinet to get some of the toys he'd purchased. When he moved to her, he looked at her nipples and his cock hardened.

"Do they hurt?" She nodded, and he reached up to take the first clamp off. "When I release them, they're going to be so sensitive that you're going to want to come. This first time, I'm going to let you because you're not used to them."

As soon as he freed her, she grabbed his arm and gripped him. Leaning down, he gently took the peak into his mouth and laved it with his tongue. She screamed out her climax as soon as he nipped at her. The other nipple was unclamped, and he did the same thing, giving her a quick but hard climax that he knew would make her shaky.

Guiding her to the hump, he leaned her over it and explained to her each thing he was doing. "I'm going to strap your wrists here, but not too tightly. What is your safe word, slave?"

"Clouds." He smacked her on the ass. "Master, my safe word is clouds."

"Very good. And when I ask you where you are in the levels of pain, what are you going to tell me?" She repeated the colors of the stop light to him and the levels. "Right. And you'll not lie to me when I ask you. You'll tell me where you are, and when you get to the red, the signal to stop, I will."

"Yes, master, you'll stop." He finished strapping her down and stood behind her. If there was a more beautiful sight, he had no idea what it was.

Taking the small feather in hand, he moved it over her ass, then down her spine. She danced on her feet as much as the straps would allow her, but she didn't speak. When she moaned, he moved the feather between her thighs and over her pussy.

"I can smell you and see your arousal. Do you have any idea what it does to me to see you like this, at my mercy?" Thad opened his pants and freed his cock. "I'm going to fuck you like this, but you're not to come. If you do, I'll punish you severely."

"Yes, master, I won't come or you're going to punish me." Thad could hear the need in her voice and moved up behind her. Her small whimper made him bring his hand down on her, but it only heightened his own need to see his handprint form on her tight ass.

Taking his cock in his fist, he moved up between her legs and rubbed his engorged head over her heat. She didn't make a sound, but he could feel her tremble. Sliding just the tip of his cock into her, he fucked her with quick, hard punches that had him wanting to come, but he pulled back before he could.

Moving to her head, he lifted her just enough to look at her. Then he pulled her head to his cock. "Suck your taste off me."

She did as she'd been told, and Thad knew he was in trouble. When she swallowed him again, he nearly came. Stepping back, he stood there for several seconds, trying his best to regain control over his body. As soon as he could move again, he leaned down and released her. Helping her stand, he reached down, ran his fingers through her wet curls, and took them to her mouth.

She watched him as she licked them clean. Yes, Thad thought, he was in big trouble.

"Go over there to the cross. It's time to show you what I do to bad girls." She didn't move for several seconds and he knew just what she was going through. The way she looked right now made him want to beg her, to let him fuck her until neither of them could move. When she finally moved, he went to the cabinet again and pulled out a small, soft whip.

Tying her to the cross was hard. His cock brushed against her every time he reached up to strap her in, and when he leaned down to tie her ankles, he bit her ass. Her reaction was a thick groan and a soft growl. Christ, he'd forgotten about her wolf.

"Will she hurt me if I play too rough?" Diamond shook her head. "I'd really hate to be killed while having the best time of my life."

"She won't. She's…she's enjoying herself too." Nodding, he moved to stand in front of Diamond to ask her about her words. "I'm to say clouds when I want you to stop completely or red when you ask. Yellow when it's almost too much, and green means I want more." She licked her lips. "Green, master, I want green."

The small whip was made of the softest leather he could find. It was made for only pleasure and not pain, but it would be painful for her and him if he denied her pleasure for very long. As soon as he stepped back to bring it down on her lovely ass, he had to pause to look at her.

Her legs were strapped to the lower half of the cross at the thighs and at her ankles. There were steps for her to stand on, and they tilted so she wouldn't cramp up. Her waist also had a wide strap around it, and it, too, was tied to the cross. The way her legs were spread out, he could move up behind her and enter her without touching her.

Her arms were over her head, and like her feet, her wrists were able to tilt for the blood circulation as well. Her wrists where strapped down, as were her upper arms. There was a wide leather strap around her neck as well, but it was purely for looks, as it wasn't attached to anything. A blindfold covered her eyes, and he knew from experience that she was going to be more excited about that than anything he actually did to her. The not knowing what he was going to do to her next was a major part of this.

Moving up behind her again, he rubbed the soft leather over her body. "I'm going to spank you with this. I'm going to beat you in places that will have you begging me to let you come. But you won't say a word." He brought it down over her ass and watched the muscle ripple from her tensing up. "Then when I've made your pretty ass ready for me, I'm going to beat you here."

This time he brought the little whip over her pussy. She cried out, but he didn't say anything. Christ, she was going to make him come all over her before he got to play. The next three times he brought it over her flesh, she didn't make a sound. When two more slapped over her pussy again, Thad started to admire her. When he brought it down over her calves, then her shoulder, he had to grip his cock or chance injuring himself. For ten minutes he moved over her body with the whip until he couldn't take it any longer.

He knew he should let her go, but the thought of taking her this way was overwhelming. Lowering her to the floor by the hydraulics, he leaned her over slightly and moved up behind her. Without a word, he slammed his cock into her wet pussy and stilled.

"You come and I'll beat you." She nodded, but didn't speak. "You're so tight and wet. I could stay here all day and never move. The thought of filling you with my cum and leaving you like this has my balls so tight against my body that I don't think I'll last much more than a few strokes."

He moved slowly, painfully as he held her hips. When he was buried deep again, he opened her ass up and looked at the pretty rosette. Next time, he promised himself, he was going to come deep in the hot tight hole and cry out her name.

"You want to come, slave?" He pumped into her twice, then a third time as sweat dripped from his forehead to her back. "Would you like to release the buildup and scream out my name?"

"Yes, master, I want that. Please." He leaned over her as she begged more. "I would like to come, master. I would love for you to allow me to come, please."

Thad's balls tightened up, and the tingle down his spine was all the warning he got before his climax roared through him. Throwing back his head, he felt a primal scream, a roar really, erupt from his lips and tear throughout the room. When he leaned over her, he sank his teeth into her shoulder and reached to her mind.

Come for me. Come now. She stiffened for about two seconds before she screamed as well. Even as he filled her body with his, she milked him, rippled around his cock until he was sure she was going to hurt him. When she came a second time, Thad licked the wound closed and stroked her through another climax that had her go lax over the cross.

Thad decided that if he died right now, he'd go knowing that he had found the love of his life. Thad Galloway hadn't just fallen in love with his mate, but he'd love her for all eternity and then some.

"I love you, Diamond." He heard her say something but wasn't sure what it was. "I have loved you all my life."

~~~

Ward stood outside the big building for five minutes before he opened the door. Flair Marketing wasn't his usual place to go, but he wanted answers and the guard at his brother's house wasn't giving him any. So, he decided to go a different route.

"Hello, may I help you?" The woman at the front desk smiled at him, and Ward decided that if nothing else, this Henson person had a good head on his shoulders for hiring. This woman looked good enough to eat.

"I'm going to need for you to let me go up and speak to Blair Henson." He glanced at the man who got off the elevator before continuing. "You have to escort me? Or do I get a badge?"

"Neither." He stared at her for several seconds until the phone on her desk rang. He waited for her to hang up. Ward was going to give her the benefit of the doubt because she more than likely didn't understand who he was.

"I think you misunderstood me," he started as soon as she hung up. "I'm Ward Galloway, and I'm going to need to get up there to Blair's office. I'm trying to be nice about it. You'll either make me a badge to get there or I'll simply tell Blair how you treated me and you'll be out on the fucking streets."

When she stood up, the man who had come off the elevator took a step toward them. When she rose her hand up, he stopped moving toward them, but he didn't move back. Ward was ready to tell her to forget it and he'd simply go up when she grabbed him by the tie and pulled him nearly over the counter.

"Listen here, you slimy rectum captain, I'm working this desk because I was asked to fill in. I don't give two shits if you're the president of the United States or fucking Ward Gobbly-gook. You'll either leave this building on your own, or so help me I'll remove you all by myself."

"Who the fuck shit in your cereal?" He should have taken a breath, he realized a second later. And when he started to step back from her, he knew that she was going to try and hurt him.

Ward never saw the other man until he was holding the woman's hand up in the air.

"Jade, will you please not kill the man in my building? We've had this talk before about you and your temper. Perhaps you should take a break." She glared at the man, then looked at him.

"He made me pissed off. Ask Allen. He saw it." Everyone turned to the older man from the elevator as he nodded. "Ward here seems to think that because he's running the place, I should simply do what he says."

That confused Ward. She didn't think she should do as he told her? He was Ward Galloway—everyone should obey him. He looked at the newcomer as he let go of the woman he'd called Jade.

"This person was rude to me. I believe it would be in your best interest to fire her. She doesn't know her place." The growl that came from the woman had him taking a step back. "See what I mean? My brother will not tolerate this sort of behavior to underlings."

"Underlings? Why you waffle-headed mother fucking asshole." He wasn't sure how she managed to get away from the big man, but it took him and the other guy to pull her off him. Ward thought the woman dangerous and said so.

"You're lucky it's her and not me." The older man, Allen, stepped in front of him and poked him in the chest as he continued. "If I were in charge, I'd take you out back and beat the shit out of you."

Ward looked at the younger man. He looked like a man who knew was things were about. He was wealthy, fit, and seemed to be the one in charge of these idiots. Putting out his hand and completely ignoring the other two, he stepped toward him.

"I'm Ward Galloway. My brother Thad and I are going to do business with this firm, I'm to understand." Ward dropped his hand when the man didn't take it. "There is no reason for all of this. I've only come here to see about getting familiar with this end of the business and to speak with my brother."

"No, what you've done is come here under falsehoods to try and wiggle your way into my company by throwing around your name as if it means shit to me. You've pissed off my sister-in-law and insulted my father." The man took a step toward him as he glared hard. "What is it you really want?"

"My brother sent me here and—" Ward found himself lifted off the floor and his feet dangling a good two feet up. He started to struggle, but the man had him so tightly held that he only managed to hurt himself.

"Blair, please put the moron down." Ward looked at the man coming up behind who he assumed was Blair as he was set back on the floor. "What the fuck are you doing here, Ward? I thought I told you to stay at the hotel and wait for the police."

"Thad?" The man nodded. "Christ, you look…where can I get a suit like that? I can have it tailored, can't I? But I'd have to have a silk shirt. I don't wear cotton unless I have to."

"I could care less what you wear or don't wear as a matter of fact. And unless you have a job somewhere, I'm not footing the bill for you to have a suit made only to wear to jail." Thad looked around the room and smiled. Ward turned to see what had changed him from being pissed off to smiling like a sap when he saw them.

Good Christ, they were beautiful. Five of the most…no make that six, because when the woman from the desk joined them, he could see that they were all related. He'd never seen so many hookers in one place in all his life.

"Are you going to share them?" He looked at Blair when he growled. "You can't think to keep all these lovely pieces of ass all to yourself. Christ man, they must be costing you a fortune if you're paying them by the hour."

The woman in the front smiled at him as she moved toward him. Now this was a way to greet a man. When she raised her hand, he reached for it only to have her snatch it back. He took a step toward her only to come up short when she grabbed his balls. Tight.

"Honey, you may want to—" Ward reached out to slap her when she tightened her grip. He felt sweat bead on his forehead when she gave him a hard twist, but he didn't touch her again.

"Ward, I'd like you to meet my future wife, Diamond. Diamond, honey this is my idiot brother. He's going to tell us why he's here and what the fuck he was thinking killing that man."

"I didn't kill anyone." Ward cried out when she twisted his balls again. "Christ, make her stop, she's hurting me."

"And she'll continue hurting you until you answer the fucking questions. Why did you kill that man?" This man could not be his brother and he started to tell him so when the woman, Diamond, twisted his balls tighter.

"He touched me. I only wanted a suit and he was going to…he was going to blow me." Diamond laughed, and that made him reach for her again. "You fucking cunt."

Ward connected with her mouth, but she pulled on his balls again before she fell back. He couldn't breathe for several seconds, but saw that while they helped her up from the floor, he was free. He limped to the door as quickly as he could, and was nearly out when someone shouted his name. Blair came at him now, and somehow he knew that if the big man caught up with him, he'd be dead. Ward crashed through the door and out into the street.

Stepping into traffic had cars horns blaring and tires squealing, but he knew that if he stopped, getting hit by a car was going to be the least of his problems. When he ran to the other side of the street, he dodged people, carts, and other displays out on the sidewalk in a blind need to get as much distance between him and Blair as he could.

Ward had no idea how far he'd gone before he simply couldn't move anymore. Leaning against the wall in a darkened alley, he tried to catch his breath and figure out what to do now. Every time a horn blared, he nearly jumped out of his skin, but he had to do something. Stepping cautiously into the street, he found himself to be in one of the worst neighborhoods he'd been in as yet, but there was a taxi, so he hailed it. As soon as he got in, he looked around and saw Blair coming up the sidewalk to where he'd been.

"Where to, buddy? Meter's running." Ward needed him to get going, so told him the mall. He had no idea if this little town had one, but figured it was his best bet. When the cab took off, Ward looked back. Blair was stepping into the alley where he'd just been. Christ, how had he found him so quickly?

When Ward was dropped off at the food court, he ordered himself a cola from the only restaurant that had a name he was familiar with and sat at one of the cleanest dirty tables he could find. He pulled out his wallet and counted what he had. There was no way he could go back to the hotel, and getting anything from Thad was going to be difficult until he could explain to him what had happened so he could get him out of this mess.

Thad would do it too. It was his responsibility to keep Ward out of jail and safe. There was no way he'd let him go to jail over some trumped up charge like murder. Ward decided to not let that worry him. But his lack of funds did.

He had less than fifty dollars left. How had that happened? he wondered. Someone had come into his hotel room and robbed him, he figured. There was no way he'd spent that much...okay, maybe he had. There had been the dinners he'd bought and the things he'd purchased for his new office, the one Thad would give him when this was straightened out. Then there were the whores he'd paid for.

"A man can't be expected to be celibate for his entire life." He realized he'd spoken out loud when the woman next to him glared. "You might be able to because of the simple fact that you're old, fat, and ugly."

Ward had to have a plan to get to talk to Thad. This would be cleared up in no time if he just told him that he loved him or some other shit. He might even be able to convince him that he was sorry. That had worked on his dad, but not so much on Thad. Thad had a way to see right through all his bullshit.

When the mall started closing up, Ward made his way to the bathroom. He'd stay there tonight. Surely they made allowances for people like him. He hid in the bathroom until he was sure everything was quiet, and then went to find a shop that had beds. Ward was suddenly very tired, and his fucking balls hurt.

Chapter 15

Thad watched the police move around the lobby of Blair's building. He wanted to go out and find the little prick and kill him himself, but didn't have a clue how to find him. Blair walked in just as he was getting up to pace.

"I lost him over on Germantown. I think he got into a cab or had a car. The trail died right there." Thad knew that as a wolf this family could find anything once they had their scent, but he was still worried about how much more damage Ward could do before he was caught.

"I thank you for trying." Blair nodded and went to his dad. Diamond sat down next to him, and he pulled her into his lap. Her small squeak made him laugh.

"Are you all right?" He didn't answer her because honestly, he wasn't sure if he was or not. "I'm sorry I let him go, but I hadn't expected him to slap me."

"He's going to pay dearly for that." He kissed the small bruise already forming. "Once you shift, will it go away?"

"Yes. Sapphire asked me to wait until later to do it so the police could see how hard he hit me. It doesn't hurt, but it is annoying that they keep pampering me about it." She snuggled up to his throat and nipped at his ear lobe. "Your little whip was more painful than his hand was."

His cock took a painful twist, and he had to move her on his lap to adjust himself. She had enjoyed their play and not only that, she'd gotten up this morning and asked him to explain what each piece of equipment did and what he would do to her in them. He'd spent a delightful hour showing her how the cockball worked.

It was on the same principle as a child's bouncy ball. It had a handle and it was made of a heavy-duty plastic. But that was where the similarities ended. This one had a cock on it. Thick and long, the rider, in this case her, would slide over it and bounce. He'd watched her come twice before he tossed her to the floor and took her from behind. Christ, he'd never came so hard in his life.

"I'm wet." Thad looked at her when she whispered in his ear. "Very wet. Feeling your cock under my ass is making me think of all kinds of things I'd like to do to you right now."

Thad stood her up, and when he was standing, jerked her along behind him as he went in search for an empty room. Any room would do so long as there was a lock on the door. The first one he opened had the police in there with Allen. Thad closed the door without a word, but could swear he heard Allen laugh.

The second one was also occupied, but he was determined. When the third room was empty, he pulled her in behind him and pressed her against the wall.

"You're going to pay for teasing me." She moaned as he took her mouth. Lifting his head, he reached down to put his hand under her skirt to see if she'd done what he'd told her. He was met with warm, wet flesh. Stroking her pussy with his fingers, Thad moved her blouse up with his free hand.

"Please, master, I want to suck your cock." He rocked into her, wondering if a man had ever died because of too much sex. When he leaned down and took her nipple into his mouth, he decided that he didn't care if he died like this or not. This was the only way to go.

"I'm going to eat you until I've had my fill. Then I'm going to fuck you. Go over to the table and spread out for me." She moved to the table, pulling her skirt up over her hips as she moved. Her ass looked good enough to eat, and Thad wanted her.

She lay back on the table and braced her feet on the edge. Thad had a perfect view of her pussy and how wet she was. When she opened her legs as wide as she could, he pulled a chair to her.

Thad thought about playing with her, but hunger for her won out. He leaned in and took her clit into his mouth. At the same time he pressed two fingers into her heat. She nearly came up off the table but didn't make a sound. With his free hand, he moved to release his cock before he hurt himself.

The cool air from the air conditioner did nothing to slow him down. He suckled her pussy and drank her down as he fisted his cock. Pre-cum dripped from the tip, and Thad used it to make the slide quicker and easier.

You taste delicious, love. He loved being able to speak to her this way. *I'm going to fuck you soon, and when I do, I want you to not make a sound when you come.*

Yes, master, not make a sound when I come. He felt her need rush over his body, and he nipped at her clit. *Please, master. Please.*

He stood up and shoved the chair away from him. Her pussy was so wet from her juices that when he entered her, it was as if he was coming home. Wrapping her legs around him, she locked them at his hips, and he leaned over the table to her mouth.

"Taste you on me." She licked his lips and suckled the lower one into his mouth as he began moving in and out of her heat. "You're mine, Diamond, all mine."

Her back bowed up, and he felt his own release racing to meet hers. As soon as she tightened around him, he pistoned into her so hard that the table began to dance across the floor. When she licked his throat, he tilted his head and gave it to her. When she bit him, it was all Thad could do not to throw back his head and howl.

The moment she tore at his throat he knew this bite was different. His balls tightened to his body again, and when she growled, he came. Dizziness swamped him as she held her mouth over his wound, and he heard her speaking to him through their link as the room began to fade in and out.

I'm so sorry. I'm so sorry. I don't know what...please don't die. Please. He held her to him as best he could as he was slipping away. Something was happening, but he didn't know what.

It's fine. I'm fine. He wasn't, and he was pretty sure they both knew it. *I'm just...I think you're doing something to me.*

Changing you, he thought she said, but that wasn't right. There had to be a mortal wound. *I'm so sorry. I didn't mean to do this to you.*

He wanted to answer her but no longer seemed to have the ability to speak. He was slipping fast, and his final thought was he'd really done it, he'd died during sex.

~~~

"What the fuck were you thinking? You could have killed him, and then what would you have done?" Diamond didn't answer him again. She'd answered him every time he'd asked her and she still didn't have a better answer.

"She's told you that she didn't mean to do it to him. Let it rest, Blair, before I get pissed off and change you into something. Unconscious is sounding really good about now." Sapphire sat beside her on the small sofa in her room. "He's going to be fine when he wakes. I'm just glad you didn't let him go when you bit him or he might have died."

Diamond had nicked his artery. She'd not meant to, but had bitten through it and when his arterial blood filled her mouth, she'd done the only thing she could think of and let her wolf go enough to change him before he bled to death. And now he lay on their bed, resting.

"What the fuck were you doing having sex in one of my offices anyway?" She flushed, and Sapphire cleared her throat at him. "It's my building. If I want to have sex with you in the open lobby, it's my right. Not hers. She's my...she's my sister, and she's not to have sex again."

"That is the stupidest thing I've ever heard you say." They all looked at the big bed where Thad was sitting up. "And if you think I'm never having sex with her again just because you said so, you're about half baked. I'm in love with her."

Diamond moved to the bed when he reached for her. She took his hand and kissed it. She could smell his wolf, and hers wanted him to come out and play. But she only held him and calmed her wolf with promises that it would be soon.

"I'm sorry. I hurt you, and it was—" He put his hand over her mouth, cutting her off.

"You changed me, didn't you?" She nodded as he didn't move his hand so she could speak. "I'm glad you did. I was going to speak to you about it, but I wasn't sure how to bring it up. Why did you do it?"

"I nicked your vein. Usually we bite the shoulder or sometimes the throat, but I'd misjudged where I was and severed the artery. It was change you or let you bleed to death. I wasn't ready for that." He kissed her mouth and laid back down, taking her with him.

Diamond looked around the room from his chest. Her sister and Blair had left. Wrapping her arms around Thad, she let the tears fall. She'd never been so afraid in her life.

"You were getting so weak I was afraid that I wasn't doing it right. Then I heard your heart beating a little stronger and then stronger still until I knew that you'd make it. I had to…we weren't dressed very well, so I had to lay you on the floor and dress you before I could call Blair in to help me get you home." She laughed a little. "He's not happy with me."

"He'll get over it." Thad kissed her head. "I remember thinking that the bite was different and that I was getting weak from it. I thought it was because I was dying from too much sex. I guess I didn't."

"No, not from that." She sat up and looked down at him. "You're a wolf now. I'm very sorry to have done it without asking you, but I didn't want you to die."

"Why?" She knew the answer but was afraid to tell him. He'd told her several times that he'd loved her during or right after sex, but this was simply the two of them. When he said her name, she got up to pace.

"I've fallen in love with you. I'm not sure when it happened or why, but I have. I guess it was when you bought me the house, but I'm sure that's not all of it. Then there is the way you've been with me. I don't mean the sex, but…." He said her name again, and she looked at him. "I'm in love with you because you're the only man in the world who never made me feel like I'm nothing."

"You're everything to me." He sat up on the edge of the bed, and she went to him. She knew he'd be weak and more than likely starving. When his belly growled, she laughed.

"I could eat a cow." She helped him stand up and guided him to the bathroom when he said he needed a shower. "I feel like I've had the flu for a week and been run over too. Does this get better soon?"

"Yes. I'm going to get into the shower with you to help you. You're going to be weak for a few hours yet, and I've had Benson make you a big dinner. I'll have him bring it up—"

"Please, I want to go outside. I feel…I need to be out of doors after this. Even if it's to just sit on the deck." He glanced at the window. "It's dark out. How long have I been here?"

"Two days." He stopped moving and stared at her. "It should have been longer, but you're just too stubborn to do things the correct way. And you should also know that Benson is aware of what we are. He knew what I was, but he's aware that you are too."

"Benson knew? What is he?" She laughed. "Let me guess, he's not a wolf but a…I was going to say tiger but that can't be right. He's a bear."

"He's a black bear. And he's very glad you know now." He stopped her from pulling his shirt over his head. "I'm not going to hurt you."

"Christ, I know that. I just wanted to tell you that I love you too. I meant to do it when you said it but you've distracted me. I love it when you wear my shirts."

"You really love me?" He kissed her on the mouth and stepped back to help her undress him. "I didn't know if you meant it when we were having sex. I thought it was because you were wrapped up in the moment."

"I was. Like I said, you distract me. But I do love you. Very much." When he was naked, she helped him into the stall with the warm water running. By the time she'd slipped in behind him, he had managed to wash his hair. He was leaning against the wall. "I'm sorry, but I'm done in. I'll need your help after all."

When he was dressed in a pair of very old sweat pants and a tee-shirt, she helped him back to bed. Sitting on the deck was going to have to wait. By the time Benson brought them up a light dinner, he was nearly asleep. She had to wake him twice to finish. When she took the tray off his lap, she started out of the room, but he called her back.

"You're going to sleep with me, aren't you? I need to know that you're here beside me even if it's only to hold you." Diamond nodded and took the tray down to the kitchen and handed it to Benson.

"Is he all right, missus?" She nodded, overwhelmed by the simple fact that he was alive and well. "You've done a great thing for him by loving him. He was so bitter those few years after his father died. The man was a horrible father and a worse husband. Mrs. Galloway died of a broken heart in the way that they treated her."

"What did they do?" He looked out the window to the yard beyond, and she was sure he wasn't going to answer her. But when he turned to look at her, she could see that he'd been a little in love with the former Mrs. Galloway.

"She was the kindest person in the world and loved her sons. Thad was a good boy and has become a better man. Ward was rotten even as a baby, and that father of his could see nothing wrong with him. Gave him the world even if it meant that Thad did without." He handed her a glass of tea and a plate of cookies. They sat at the table.

"They were always rich then?" He shook his head. "I thought…I assumed that Thad inherited his money from his family."

"Oh no, missus, he is a self-made man. When I first came to work for him after he started making money, the first thing he said to me was to not lend or give anything that I valued to his father or brother. I never did, but I saw how they treated him. Mr. Thad worked a great deal, and the more he made the more they wanted. His mother passed when Mr. Thad had been in high school, and his father…his family moved in with him right after, sucking him as dry as he'd let them. Then when the mister died, Mr. Thad set some rules up for the brother, but by then it was too late. He already had a taste for having things his way."

Diamond got up and poured them both refills of tea and sat down again before she spoke. "Ward was rude to Jade. She said if she ever saw him again she'd murder him. Did you know that he killed that man in Texas?"

"I did, missus. I did. Shame that someone had to die for him to get what he deserved, but the boy has always been bad. I don't know what would have happened if Mr. Thad had not tossed him out that day. He'd taken so much from him. I think it...I believe Mr. Thad was more hurt by it than he'd ever say."

Diamond was sure he was right. "Thad said I could take things from the house in Texas that I thought I'd want. Other than his mother's things, can you think of anything that I should have sent to me?"

When he flushed slightly, she wondered if he knew about Thad's playroom and decided that if he did he wouldn't tell her. Instead, he pulled out his phone and showed her several pictures.

"It's his crib, missus. I had...I unearthed it one day when I was cleaning. I had it put into the attic and made sure that no one but me knew it was there. The last Mrs. Galloway's brother had given it to his sister as a baby gift. She said that he carved it for her."

The crib was beautiful and lovingly put together. She enlarged the picture and looked up at Benson, startled. He nodded once and went to the sink to wash up their glasses.

There were animals carved into the headboard as well as the footboard. And when she looked harder, she noticed that they were wolves at play. Most of them were a little hard to see, but she could see clearly what they were. Someone, a long time ago, had carved wolves into the bed. That's when she remembered that before she'd changed him, Thad had the ability to seal wounds.

"I think his great-grandfather was mated to a wolf. No one ever said, but as a supe I can see things like you can." Benson never turned as he continued at the sink. "I've a feeling that Mr. Thad is more wolf than human. What do you think?"

"I think so too." And she knew that they were talking more about before he'd been converted. Diamond started to remember a few other things that had startled her about Thad and wondered if what Benson said was true. He really was part wolf.

After they cleaned up the kitchen a little, she went back up to bed. Thad was still sleeping, so she crawled into bed with him, not bothering with finding something to pull on. She was almost asleep before her head hit the pillow.

Chapter 16

Ward was slowly running out of options. His money was all but gone, and he was still staying at the mall after three days. He was sure that soon he'd be caught, and no matter how much he begged them to call Thad to bail him out, he had a feeling that he'd let him rot. He was quickly becoming disappointed in his older brother.

Thad had never been very nice to him. And he only gave in to him when Ward had gone to their dad. Now there was a man who loved him. Dad gave him everything, and never once in all his life did his dad ever tell him no. Thad had been mean to do what he'd done about throwing him out of the house, and it was worse yet that he'd waited until Dad was dead before he'd done it. Ward wandered around the food court, trying to decide if he could get anyone to give him something to eat. It hadn't worked so far.

But his plan was coming together. Slowly, but it was coming. He sat at one of the tables in the food court and thought about what he'd discovered just last night. There were guns here. He'd been in the shower that was some sort of break room for the guards when he heard someone come in. Luckily, he'd been drying off or the man might have caught him at his bath. As it was, he'd had to jump in a toilet stall and wait for the man to start singing before he moved out.

The man's clothes had been lying across the bench, and in his open locker was a wallet with only about seventy bucks, as well as a key. Ward took both the cash and the key, wondering if he could figure out where it went. By the time the man had come out and was dressing, Ward had not only discovered what it unlocked but had also found the lost and found, where there was even more cash.

But that hadn't lasted long. After he'd bought himself a new shirt and nice watch that told the time in five countries, he was broke again. He felt as if he was never going to get anything the way money seemed to just disappear on him. But he'd taken a knife, as well as put the gun where he could find it. And now he was thinking it was time to take care of things.

His plan was to borrow some money from one of the drawers in the busiest restaurant here. He'd already discovered that none of the stores, especially the bigger ones, had any cash around. But he figured that someone would have cash at the register. It was only until he could get Thad to pay up.

"He's just too selfish for a man with all the money." Ward looked around when he'd realized he'd spoken out loud, and decided to take another walk about the place. But Thad had always been this way with his things. His clothes as well as his cars, things that Thad had bought because he'd had a job. Not even his dad could make him share that shit. Not that Ward had wanted it all that much. But it was the principle of the thing.

Ward smiled when he thought of the time he'd taken his car out for a joy ride. He figured that Thad had wanted him to do it or he wouldn't have left the keys out where he could find them. And he'd had to look hard for them, too, if he remembered correctly.

But the crowning jewel had been when he'd managed to take all that money. Of course, he'd had to lose all he'd bought with it, but that, too, was his brother's fault. How he found him was anyone's guess, unless that fucking cunt Jane had told him. She'd been a burr up his ass since he'd been a teenager. She always seemed to know just when he was up to something. And that fucking bastard Benson. That man would rather have died than to lend him any money, and Ward knew that he made enough. None of the people in the house that Thad had bought would do anything for him. It was as if they knew he wasn't going to pay them back. Ward stopped moving, and a woman bumped into him from behind.

"He told them not to. Fucking bastard told them all to not lend me a dime. Mother fuck." Ward was walking around the court again when he thought of something else. "He said that that woman was his future wife. She'll get it all if Thad dies. Probably have him milked dry before I get the chance to anyway."

The more he thought about it the more pissed off he got. What was her name…something like a stone or something? Ward was walking by the jewelry store when it occurred to him, Jade, her name was Jade. "Or some other bullshit."

When he rounded to the food court again, he used his last couple of dollars to buy him a burger and fries. Water was free, so he had a glass of it rather than a bottle and hated the fact that they'd reduced him to this. He'd be on top again, and when he was, Ward decided that everyone was going to remember his name and what he stood for or else.

By the time the mall was closing down, he had things worked out in his head. He'd get enough money to get a cab out to his brother's place, rob him or make him give him some money, then sit him down and have a long talk about what he expect from him. It wasn't much…a house for starters.

Not like the one he had, but almost. Ward also wanted a staff to run it and keep it neat. As much as he despised filth, he didn't want to have to clean up after himself either. Then there was a car. He decided that he'd want a limo and a driver on call all the time. He didn't want to have to wait on someone to come and pick him up. Then there were the credit cards.

Ward thought that as Thad's brother he should have as much to spend as he wanted. It wasn't as if Thad spent all that much. The man did not know how to live as far as Ward could see. He'd had on a nice suit, of course, but his shirt had been a cotton one, and if Ward wasn't mistaken, it had been a simple tee-shirt and not silk like he should be wearing. A man should wear silk all the time. And then there was the girlfriend. She'd have to go.

Yes, she was beautiful and all, but she was from the working class. Blair seemed like a nice man, but he worked for a living, and those types of riffraff did not mingle with his kind. Ward wondered why Thad had never known about these rules of the rich and shook his head. After about a month of hanging out with him, the new Thad would be someone to reckon with.

Slipping into the bathroom, he pulled his feet up on the seat and waited. It was annoying to have to do this nightly, but after today, he was going to be living in style. As he waited for the building to close down, he thought maybe as his last night as a guest here he'd make it worth his while. Yes sir, he was going to make sure that when the place opened up in the morning, they were going to be scratching their heads over his gift to them for months.

~~~

"I've packed up all the things that Mrs. Galloway wanted, as well as had the few things that Benson suggested sent along too. The women that are going to take my place are going to run the business down here for a few short days while I'm up there. Then when I return, I'll go over everything with them to see how they did." Thad was making notes as quickly as Jane spoke. He'd been on the phone with her for over an hour, and it didn't look like they were making much in the way of progress. Benson entered with a tray and sat a cup of coffee in front of him as well as an envelope. He opened it as Jane went on about hiring more staff for the Texas plant.

"Whoever you hire, make sure they are well aware that if the company moves, they will have first option of taking a job here." The note was from Diamond. He read it before continuing with Jane.

I went to the hospital to get my office straightened out. There are some things I want to discuss with you when I get home. Do you think we can do something about a fundraiser for the hospital? Love, your diamond in the rough.

He added that to his growing list of things to get started. Thad also put on the list "run with Diamond" and underlined it several times.

"The new guy I interviewed has some great ideas. I'd like for you to come down and arrange to meet him before I make a job offer." He didn't have time for that.

"You like him?" Jane said she did and thought he was a good fit. "Then give him the job and tell him that in a few weeks I'll need him to come up here and help with the layout of the new plant. Also, make sure you have him keep an eye out for his replacement. If he's that good, I want him with my best team up here with us."

"Okay. There is the matter of the family that your brother murdered. I've sent the money, as you've asked, as well as paid for whatever they had in way of a funeral. They want to meet with you as well. Thank you for everything, they said. Before you ask, yeah, I've made sure that they keep all the information about the donations and money to themselves too." Thad decided that Jane needed a raise and wrote that on his list at the top. "I've been looking at houses and was wondering if they really are that cheap up there. I mean, the place I have now is about half the size as the ones up there, but they're nowhere near what I paid for mine. Seriously?"

"Seriously. When you come up in a few days, we'll take you around. You can stay here while you're looking, and that way you can take your time. Besides, Diamond wants to get to know you. She said she's never met a vamp before."

After he hung up the phone with her, he went to find Benson. He was starving. Before he could ask, Benson handed him a platter of food and told him to sit. He was about halfway finished when he sat across from him.

"The missus said for me to call her Diamond. I was wondering how I can tell her that it isn't done." Thad looked at his cook of the past twelve years and smiled. "You're going to tell me to call her Diamond and be done with it, aren't you?"

"I think you'll live longer if you do." He picked up the glass of tea that Benson handed him. "I don't know how I lived without her before this. And while we're on the subject, I think if you call me Mr. Thad once more I might brain you. It's Thad...it's always been Thad."

Benson nodded. "The matter of the house, sir. I'm not sure—" After a heavy sigh, Benson shook his head. "I will move in as soon as the painters are finished. Your missus is hard to reason with, is she not?"

"No, not really. I don't reason with her at all. She says what she wants, and I do my best to get it for her. She's not really demanding and asks for very little, so when she asks, I know it's something she really wants." Thad sat back in his chair and looked around the kitchen that was in various stages of remodel. "Like this kitchen. You said it was fine. What changed your mind?"

Benson flushed and stood up. "I'll be picking up the missus from the hospital at two, sir. Then from there we are headed to the mall for some shopping. She said she needs my help on a dress to wear to the ground breaking on Friday."

Thad let it go, knowing that Diamond had convinced Benson that he needed a nicer kitchen by simply smiling at him. It worked on him as well. Thad remembered the fundraiser.

After about an hour of going over what was going to go into having a fundraiser here at the house, Thad went out onto the deck and looked at the woods. He wanted to run again. Yesterday, after they'd made love twice before coming downstairs, she'd taken him out and helped him shift. It was the most amazing thing he'd ever done. Then they'd run through the woods for an hour before he'd needed to come in for a call. It was still amazing to him how much his body had changed, and so much for the better. He felt her touch his mind.

There have been some problems at the mall. Turn on the news. He moved to enter the house again as Benson was coming out. The television in the kitchen was already on. He pulled out his cell phone to call her.

"They're saying they have a lead on who it was. I'm talking to a friend of mine at the police station, and he's telling me it's a man by the name of Galloway, as if we didn't already know that. He signed everything he did. What a moron." He watched as the camera crew walked around all the destruction his brother had caused. "There were some break-ins in two of the restaurants as well. Apparently, when he couldn't find whatever it was he was looking for, he turned on the fryers and had himself a meal, then set fire to the kitchen area in one of the places."

"Money. He's been looking for money. Are you still at the hospital?" She said she was. "Please stay there. I don't know if he'll come there or not, but I'd rather you were someplace safe."

"I'll stay, but you have to do that as well. If he was looking for money and didn't find any, he might come looking for you next." He thought she was right. "Thad, do you think he'll kill anyone else?"

"I don't know, honey. I really don't." He watched the news for another twenty minutes before he went back to his office. Benson told him he'd keep him updated on things, and Thad started looking over the plans for the new building. Groundbreaking was in just a few days, and his brother was going to fuck it up, he just knew it. As he was sitting there trying to work out one of the issues that kept coming up in his other plant, Benson walked in. Thad started to say something when he realized he wasn't alone. Ward had him at gunpoint.

"Hello, brother dear. I bet you didn't expect to see me here." Benson sat down in the chair across from his desk, and that's when Thad noticed the blood. He asked him what had happened.

"I was making my way to the garage, sir, when he hit me from behind. I was out for only a few seconds, but it was enough for him to get the jump on me. I do apologize, sir." Benson put his handkerchief to his head and winked. "I do feel the most faint when I'm unable to sit, sir. I was wondering...do you think it possible that I have a cold drink?"

"Shut the fuck up." Ignoring Ward, Thad went to the small refrigerator near the file cabinet and got a bottle. He wasn't sure what Benson wanted from him until he was right there. On top of the cabinet was the camera that he and Benson had been playing with earlier. It had come with the house. They'd found it and the bank of recorders in one of the wall closets in this room. He pressed the button to record his brother.

"What are you doing here, Ward? The police are looking for you." His brother snarled at him. "You think I'm going to bail you out of this, you're stupider than I thought."

"Why don't you just give me what I want?" Thad was surprised by the outburst and laughed. "I want you to give me what I had before. An office at your new building and a house. I don't want an apartment this time, a real house. With a staff. I'm not going to clean up after myself when you can afford to have it done for me."

"Anything else while you're making demands?" Thad reached for Blair. He nearly reached for Diamond, but he was afraid she'd get hurt, and he didn't want that. Blair said he was on his way.

Diamond said she could feel that you were upset and tried to call the house. She said Benson alerted her that Ward was there. He'd have to find out what they'd said to each other. *I've called the police, too, but I don't think they're going to be there before me.*

More than likely not. He looked at Ward, then Thad realized he was waiting for an answer. "I'm not going to give you anything. I'm not going to pay off any of the places you destroyed, nor am I going to pay for a lawyer. I hope you end up in jail for a very long time."

"What is wrong with you? How can you live here with that woman and not want more?" Ward got up to pace but kept his gun near Benson. "I've been trying and trying to show you what you need, but you continue to want to shun the type of lifestyle that you were born to."

"I was born to a poor family the same as you were. My mother worked her ass off all day to come home and fix dinner for Dad, who rarely came home from one of the women he was seeing to eat with us. Dad never left the couch to even find a job, and when he did, he was usually fired within a few weeks for being drunk on the job." Thad leaned back in his chair. "I've worked very hard for what I've got, and I see no reason whatsoever to give any of it to you. You want money, find a job, a real job."

"But I'm your brother." Thad waited for him to say more, but apparently he thought that should explain it. He shook his head. There was something seriously wrong with his brother.

177

"What about that man you killed in Texas? What do you have to say about that?" His brother started pacing again, and Thad noticed that he was talking to himself. He could hear him but didn't understand what he was saying.

"He touched me. My person, and that is just not what is done to a person of my caliber. I'm Ward Galloway, and Ward Galloway is rich. Rich men do not get blow jobs from underlings." Ward turned to look at him. "He was a ways to a means. I needed money, and he had it. What other reason could there be?"

"You murdered a man in cold blood for his money?" Thad knew his brother was sick, but this was beyond what he'd thought he'd say. "You simply needed something and took it? Damn the consequences?"

"Of course. Isn't that what I've been trying to tell you to do for the past twenty minutes? You can fuck that Jade woman, but don't fucking marry her. She's not worthy of you."

"Jade? What does Jade have to do with this?" He tried to remember how she'd been involved in all this, and remembered the encounter at Blair's office. "I'm not marrying Jade." His brother sagged with relief.

"Thank God. She's well beneath you, and you should have seen it well before now. No matter, we'll get this all straightened out and I'll make sure it never happens again." His brother put the gun in his pants and walked toward him. "You'll see, things will go better now that I'm going to be working here."

"I'm marrying her sister, Diamond. And you won't be working here either." Thad reached out and grabbed his brother's extended hand. He was more than likely going to shake on the deal, but Thad had had enough. With a quick twist, he had his brother down on the desk and Benson was disarming him.

"I thought for sure he'd never shut up." Thad laughed at Benson. "Sire, if you don't mind me saying so, I think your brother has delusions of grandeur that are simply insane."

Thad couldn't have agreed more.

Chapter 17

"I do hope you're happy." Diamond turned to see Jan standing behind her. "You've gotten me written up and put on probation. If one more nurse complains, I'm going to lose my job. All because of you."

"Doubtful that it's because of me. You should have taken better care of the people who support you and not run them into the ground." Diamond hung the last picture on the wall to her new office before going to her desk. "I'm going to make sure that all the nurses, new and old, know that they're not your whipping posts and will be respected." Jan huffed, sat down in the chair across from her, and looked around.

The office wasn't anything Diamond had expected. It was on the fourth floor and was so lovely that she spent an hour when she'd arrived today just wandering around it. Thad had given her a big desk as well as the lovely chair she was looking forward to using, and Blair had given her a computer as well as a nice printer. She was set up. Even Sapphire had designed and printed her business cards that seemed to be burning a hole in her pocket to hand out. When Jan looked at her, she didn't look any happier.

"Nice office. Who did you have to blow to get it?" Diamond didn't answer, but she did think about pressing the button on her desk to alert security as soon as she sat down. But she couldn't find it. There was no way she was putting up with this abuse any longer.

"I want you to leave. I've contacted security and I'm going to report you to the—" Jan pulled a gun out and pointed it at her. "That's not necessary. You're not only going to lose your job but your license too if you pull that trigger."

"It's a done deal now. As of this morning as a matter of fact, when I lost my temper in the nurses' lounge. But they've all decided that they want to follow rules now and not help me out when I tell them I need them. You turned them all against me, and your sister went up and reported me already. What did you do, tell her to watch me so that my first little mistake, she would get rid of me? I really hate you Erickson women, all of you. Well, if I go so do you."

Diamond wasn't afraid, but she was concerned. If she pulled the trigger, not only might she get hurt, but Diamond was having a hard time calming her wolf. She wanted out to take care of this woman, and she was afraid that she would do it. She reached for Thad, hoping he was still close enough to help her.

Thad, are you still in the hospital? If you are, do you think you can come to my office right now? I have a situation.

His laughter hummed along her skin. *You need me to come up there and show you what I meant about bending you over the desk? I assure you that it's going to take me the rest of the day to get it just right. I might even have to continue showing you when I get home—*

Jan is in my office, and she has a gun pointed at me. I'm not really afraid, but I would very much like it if you came up here and helped me out. She felt his terror. *It'll be all right, I promise you. Just come up, okay?*

He told her he was on his way, and she could feel Blair sort of knocking at her mind. She told him what she told Thad, and he said he was coming as well. She just hoped that neither of them was hurt by this woman. Her wolf wouldn't be contained if they were.

She'd tried to be calm, but the woman didn't look like she had much to lose and was going to kill her. There wasn't silver in the gun, but a bullet to the head was pretty permanent and she wasn't ready to die right now. When there was a brisk knock at her door, she nearly stood up to let them in when it suddenly burst open. Thad stood there as a sleek, black wolf.

"I'd put that down if I were you. I'm pretty sure he is a great deal faster, and if he gets to you, he will tear your throat out." Jan stared at Thad but didn't put her gun down. "Jan, if you shoot him, you're going to piss me off and I'll shift too. You'll never survive the two of us."

"Where did you get that...what the hell is a dog doing in my hospital?" Jan shifted the gun to Thad, who growled at her. "What the hell is that thing doing here? And what do you mean 'shift too'?"

"I'm a wolf too, and mine is really going to hurt you if you shoot at him. He won't die, but he will be really pissed off." Jan turned to look at her, but the gun was still on Thad. "You shoot him and I shit you not, I'll tear your throat out so fast it wouldn't matter if you were in the operating room to be repaired, you'll be dead."

"This can't be happening. Wolves do not run free in the hospital." Diamond could see Thad moving into the room slowly while Jan continued. "I just wanted to be a good doctor and make people know that I'm important. I am, too. I graduated at the top of my class, and you stupid nurses should respect me. I'm not going to go down easy."

Thad was behind Jan's chair when Diamond spoke. "You're babbling, and I, for one, have no idea why you think we should respect you when you've never done the same to us. You're nothing but a bully, and you're getting just what you deserve."

The gun went off just as Thad leapt at Jan. The room vibrated with the sound, and before Diamond could shift as well, if that was her intention, Jan was lying on the floor with her throat covered in Thad's massive jaws. If she moved or did anything stupid now, she was as good as dead. Finally finding the stupid button, Diamond pressed it several times just as she moved around her desk to kneel down beside her on the floor. This was not going to go well, she just knew it. Thad had his paw on her chest as well, holding her still.

"I warned you." Diamond moved the gun away from her hand and left it close in the event she needed it. "This is going to be how this works. And so you know, I hope you fuck up because I'd like nothing better than to have him tear your throat out right now."

I'm shot, love. Not in any place that I think will kill me, but my leg, my rear one, is hurting like a motherfucker. Do you think we could...Christ, it's not silver is it? Diamond heard the panic in his voice.

No, it's just a plain bullet, but if you bleed on my nice carpet I'm going to make you pay. She was so afraid for him, but when he laughed, she felt so much better. *Are you all right?*

"Yes, I am. Now that I know you're safe. Just let's get this bitch taken care of. I want to break in your new desk. She felt the warmth of his words and glanced at her broken door, knowing that at any moment security was going to come in.

I don't think it's going to be today. There is a mad woman on my floor and a wolf at her throat. I think it'll be a while before either of us will be doing anything like that. I love you, Thad. As soon as he let Jan go, Diamond picked up the gun and pointed it at her as she stood up. *"They'll never believe you."*

"They won't believe there's a dog in the hospital? They will if I tell them. I may not be respected, but I do have some pull left." Diamond shook her head. "You're a fucking cunt, do you know that?"

The first guard came through the door just as Jan started screaming. Thad had gone to the bathroom, so no one searched for the giant motherfucking dog, as Jan kept screaming about. She was being cuffed just as Blair came into the room, and he moved to the bathroom and tossed in a small bag before coming to hold her. Thad came out and stood there staring at her, wearing a pair of scrubs as she held onto Blair. She'd never been so relieved or happy in all her life, and as she walked to him, he smiled at her. She hugged Thad to her just as the police arrived.

As Jan was being taken away, the police looked at her, she supposed for some sort of direction. Shrugging, Diamond never looked at anyone but the one cop she knew was a shifter. He winked at her just before he walked out of the room with Jan in cuffs. There would be no more talk of a giant dog running free in the hospital.

"You should know that I'm not at all happy about this." Both she and Thad looked at Blair as he continued. "First of all, there are all sorts of things you could have done without shifting in a public place, and secondly, telling me to be calm several times when I knew you weren't is not very nice. I need you both to pledge to me so that I can skip all this finding out after the fact what's going on."

"I told you what was going on." Blair shook his head at her. "Okay, you contacted me first, but I still told you."

"So you did, but would you have done it before either of you were killed? Doubtful. And my big contribution to this was to steal some clothes from the cart down the hall so your boyfriend there wouldn't be naked when the police arrived." Blair shook his head again. "Please pledge to me. I need to know when you might need me."

She thought about telling him she always needed him, but didn't. Sitting down in the chair at her desk, she was scooped up by Thad, then was sitting on his lap before she could speak. He held her tightly as he looked at Blair.

"I'll pledge to you if she does." She looked at Thad as he continued speaking to her. "We both know that as our alpha, he can demand that we pledge, but he's asking. And what will it cost us to pledge to him? Nothing. But we gain more. There are things that we can have with this connection that most humans never attain in the world. Most of which, as he's pointed out, help."

"He'll know everything. Our depression, happiness, not to mention, he'll know when we are fighting." Thad shrugged. "You don't understand, he'll know it all."

"And what is wrong with that? I doubt that he'll come running over when we have a fight. And according to the book I read, there is no way for him to know what we're saying to each other unless we want him to. As for our depression, I might want him to bring me out of my funk. But to be honest with you, Diamond, I doubt very much I'll be there again. You've made me the happiest man in the world."

She flushed at him, and he smiled. "You just want him to go away so we can have sex on this desk."

Blair stood up as he spoke. "I'm out of here. Too much information. But I would like very much for you two to think about it."

After he left, Thad held her while neither of them spoke. When she felt her eyes drift shut, she snuggled deeper into his arms until she let her body relax. Nothing in this world could have made her feel like she did right at that moment. And as sleep took her, she thought she heard him say that he loved her.

~~~

Thad watched Diamond sleep. She was his world now, and he wanted to prove how much he loved her more and more daily.

As soon as he was sure she was sound asleep, he shifted her in his arms and lifted her up. Laying her on the couch was easy, but letting her go wasn't. When she opened her eyes and looked at him, he felt himself fall over into the "Christ, I can't live without you" phase and over into the "I'll die without you" kind of love.

"You are the best thing that has ever happened to me." Thad smiled as she continued talking softly to him. "I want to spend the rest of my life trying to show you how much I love you."

"And I love you too. I want to be a better person because of you." She touched her fingers to his face and he kissed them. "Oh Diamond, do you have any idea what you do to me every time I look at you?"

"Yes, I think I do." Sitting up, he leaned back on his heels and watched her. "I'd very much like to break in my desk now. I have a need to scream out your name while you take me hard."

"I'm going to take you home first. I had a package delivered today, and I want to set it up and try it out. There are all sorts of things we can do there that we can't here. Not with a broken door anyway." He could smell her arousal and thought about what he was going to do to her when he tied her to the new chair, and realized he'd never make it. "I've decided that you'll have to service me first. I want you to sit there and suck my cock until I come down the back of your throat."

Thad stood up and moved between her legs when she sat up. He watched her move her hands up his thighs to his string on his pants, and nearly swallowed his tongue when she pulled them down with her teeth. As she pulled his pants down to his thighs, Thad curled his fingers into her hair to watch her.

As soon as his cock was free, she licked him from root to tip and then swirled her tongue around his thick head. Christ, he was ready to come right now, and his balls tightened close to his body. As soon as she took him into her mouth, he nearly let his fast approaching climax go.

Diamond didn't slow at all once he started to fuck her mouth. She took him as deep as he had ever been, and knew that if she kept this up he'd be finished long before he wanted to be. But there was no way he was going to ask her to stop, and when she swallowed around him, he knew that he was a goner.

"Open your mouth." She leaned back just a little as he fisted his cock. "Christ, you look delicious. I'm coming."

His first stream of cum splashed over her mouth and then down her chin. Every time he fisted up and down his cock, more and more of his cum sprayed over her face. Each time his cum landed near her lips, she licked it into her mouth and moaned. Christ, he'd never seen anything more sexy or beautiful. As soon as he felt his balls empty, he put his hand on the wall behind her and held on. Her tongue along his shaft had him shiver as his cock hardened again.

"Stand up at the desk. I've decided I can't wait for you to get home. I need to mark you now." She stood up, wrapped her hand around his cock, and stroked him. "You're going to pay for that."

Her smile made him think she didn't care, but when she moved to the desk and leaned over it, he decided that he didn't care. For now anyway. Moving up behind her, he pulled her to him and moved her head to the desktop. As soon he had her in the position he wanted her, he pulled her pants down to her thighs. She was gloriously naked beneath her uniform. He brought his hand down hard over her ass, and she moaned.

"You've not been very obedient, have you?" Her quiet "no master" had his cock jerk. "I'm going to have to show you who is master and who is slave."

"Yes, master, I've been very bad and need to be punished." Thad leaned over her and pressed his cock against her tight hole. When she didn't stiffen, he nearly entered her, but knew that she'd hurt now. But that didn't mean he couldn't play.

While not breaking through, he did ache to be deep inside of her. Reaching around to her pussy, he slid his fingers through her wet curls and brought them to her mouth. She suckled them like she had his cock, thoroughly and hard. He had to stop this now or he was going to come too soon.

"I'm going to fuck you, and if you come I'll deny you for a month. Do you understand?" She nodded and repeated what he'd said. "I want to fuck you until you can't move. Then when I come in you, I'm going to step back and you're to get dressed."

"Yes, master." Her voice was heavy with need, and he wanted more. Moving to her pussy by fisting his cock, Thad could feel her heat as it almost sucked him in. As soon as he was deep inside of her, he stopped moving.

"You come and I will punish you. You'll think that my hand over your ass will be a feather before I'm finished with you." He moved slowly in and out of her. "Your pussy is so wet for me. And hot. I may be here for hours yet."

Thad felt the sweat move down his spine and knew that he'd be lucky if he lasted for more than a minute, much less an hour. As he moved over and over, he could see her fingers grip the edge of the desk, and he had to smile. She was good at being his sub, but he still wanted to make her suffer just a little. Reaching to her pussy with his fingers again, he slid his finger into her and felt the slide of his cock as he fucked her.

"You're so tight around me. I love the feel of your sheath as it takes me." She shifted but didn't say anything. "Do you have any idea how much I want to tie you up and eat you until I'm so full that I can't move?"

"Please, master. Come for me." It was a breach in their play, but it had the desired effect. As soon as he moved into her again, he felt his climax roar out of him and into her. It seemed to last for hours instead of the minutes he knew it to be as he filled her with himself. As he felt the last of his cum leave his body, he nuzzled her neck and bit hard into her shoulder. Blood filled his mouth and something more. He lifted his head to look at her.

"I'm in heat." Her words spoken roughly made his wolf stir hard against his skin. "If we keep this up over the next few days, I'll conceive."

"You mean have a child?" She nodded. He moved from her body and turned her around. His pants, as were hers, were tangled around their legs, but he didn't care.

"We've never talked about children. I'm sorry. I should have told you before. Then you could have...I don't know, taken precautions."

"I want a child with you. As many as we can." She looked away, and he brought her back to look at him with his finger. "You don't want to have children?"

"I do. I want...are you sure? I mean it might be too late, but if you want to wait, we'll have to stop—" He kissed her quiet.

"How long before you know that you're having our child?" She grinned at him, and he smiled back. "You know already, don't you?"

"No, but we will when it happens. So will anyone who can smell me." He nodded. "Are you sure about this?"

"I've never been more sure about anything in my entire life." He kissed her again before he lifted her into his arms. "You, my dear, will need to marry me before this event happens. I want our child to have all he can right from the beginning."

"And if it's a girl? What do you plan to do for her?" When she stood up again and adjusted her clothes, he watched her, thinking about her belly filling with a child. Sitting in the chair, he pulled her to him and lifted her shirt to kiss her there.

"She'll be too much like her mother to want anything from me, but she'll have anything she wants." Thad looked up at her. "I love you so very much."

"And I love you too. Can we go home now?" He stood up, and after she returned from the bathroom, he stood there watching her. "What?"

"Nothing. I just can't believe how lucky I am right now." And he was too. Thad Galloway was the happiest man in the world.

About the Author

Kathi Barton, author of the bestselling series Force of Nature, lives in Nashport, Ohio with her husband Paul. In addition to writing full time Kathi likes to spend time with her eight grandkids, three children and three children-in-laws. She writes to relax and have fun.

Her muse, a cross between Jimmy Stewart and Hugh Jackman brings them to life for her readers in a way that has them coming back time and again for more. Her favorite genre is paranormal romance with a great deal of spice. You can visit Kathi on line and drop her an email if you'd like. She loves hearing from her fans. aaronskiss@gmail.com.

Follow Kathi on her blog:
http://kathisbartonauthor.blogspot.com/